DATE DUE

1/20/12			

National-Louis University
UNIVERSITY LIBRARY

5202 Old Orchard Road
Skokie, IL 60077

BROKEN MOON

Also by Kim Antieau

Mercy, Unbound

BROKEN MOON

KIM ANTIEAU

MARGARET K. McELDERRY BOOKS
New York   London   Toronto   Sydney

Margaret K. McElderry Books

An imprint of Simon & Schuster Children's Publishing Division

1230 Avenue of the Americas, New York, New York 10020

Book design by Debra Sfetsios

The text for this book is set in Bell MT and Kabel BT.

Manufactured in the United States of America

10 9 8 7 6 5 4 3 2 1

Library of Congress Cataloging-in-Publication Data

Antieau, Kim.

Broken moon / Kim Antieau.—1st ed.

p. cm.

Summary: When her little brother is kidnapped and taken from Pakistan to race camels in the desert, eighteen-year-old Nadira overcomes her own past abuse and, dressed as a boy and armed with knowledge of the powerful storytelling of the legendary Scheherazade, is determined to find and rescue him.

ISBN-13: 978-1-4169-1767-0 (hardcover)

ISBN-10: 1-4169-1767-5 (hardcover)

[1. Kidnapping—Fiction. 2. Brothers and sisters—Fiction. 3. Pakistan—Fiction. 4. Scheherazade (Legendary character)—Fiction. 5. Camel racing—Fiction.] I. Title.

PZ7.A62937Bro 2007

[Fic]—dc22   2006003780

FIRST
EDITION

For Agica,
who would have done the same

Thank you to Asma Yasmine Shafi for answering my questions about a girl's life in Pakistan. Thank you also to my sister, Michelle Antieau, who first told me about the real-life "kid jockeys." We never know what story might save a life, change a life, or change the world, so we need to keep on telling them.

PART ONE

Remember Shahrazad

May 30

DEAR LITTLE BROTHER, YOU WHISPERED when you gave me this pale green book with the blank pages. You didn't want Uncle Rubel and our mother to hear us talking. I don't know why. Ami wouldn't care. But Uncle Rubel? Is he mean to you when I am away? At least he gives us a place to live. I don't want to speak ill of any of our relations, of course, but I am not certain Baba liked him either. I miss our father so much. Will we ever get used to him being gone, Umar?

I wish you remembered when we lived in the village, before the bad thing happened and we had to move to Karachi. Baba owned a store and was well respected. We had a house. It was small, but I had my own room. At this time of year, you could smell the wildflowers that grew in a small patch near the spring, especially these blue flowers shaped like bells. Ami called them bluebells, and Baba would laugh and ask if she could hear them ringing. Ami had several saris and dupattas then—made from the softest silks, with the most becoming colors. She was much admired, our mother. But then our brother Rahman was accused, and I got hurt. That is not the story you want to hear tonight, though, is it? You wanted me to write stories about my life in Begum Naseem's house (where I work as a servant) and then read them to you when I visit on my day off.

I will try to do that, little brother. You are only six years old. I know you will not like hearing this, but you are too young for some things. Like the story of how I got hurt—even though you are the only person I have ever let touch the scar on my face. You said, "It looks like the new moon we watch for at the end of Ramadan." You grinned. "That's the time when we get to feast and celebrate. Just like I celebrate every time you come home!" And you asked if it hurt. I told you no, but it does hurt. Every time I look

in the mirror—which is not often—and I move my
dupatta away from my cheek, my heart hurts to see
what they did to me.

Why am I talking about this? It must be Uncle
Rubel. I do not want to be unkind, Umar, but he reminds
me of the men from the village. And that makes me
shudder. I don't like him talking to Ami about money. I
give her all my pay, little as it is. It must be enough to
pay for you both, plus our brothers send money. Or they
used to. I am not certain now what they do.

Anyway, you gave me the little green book and
showed me your little red book. I wonder how long it
was before he died that Baba packed the books in the
bottom of that box where you found them today. Baba
had written "Nadira" on the first blank page of my book
and "Umar" on the first blank page of your book.
"Remember Shahrazad," he wrote to me in the green
book. "Learn wisely," he wrote to you in the red book.
Do you think he knew he was going to die? It was very
hard for him to lose everything. I was only thirteen
when we left the village. He tried for four years to make
our life better here. I think it hurt him that our brothers

did not come home to help. Maybe they never realized how bad things had gotten.

I don't think I will read you everything I write here. I am writing too many sad things, even though I don't feel sad. Fatima, another servant here, is snoring next to me. I should be sleeping, but I am remembering telling you stories tonight before I left, like Baba used to tell me when I was your age. He taught me to read and write, too. I hope Ami sends you to school and doesn't listen to Uncle Rubel. You should not be working at your age! Whatever happens, I will make certain you learn to read and write. Fatima found me a pencil to use to write in this little green book. I can hide it in the book and put both in my pocket.

Tonight I told you the story of Shahrazad, the very wise and beautiful woman who saved herself and all the young women of the kingdom. The King was mad with grief because his first wife betrayed him. He would not risk another betrayal, so he took a new wife each night and had the new wife killed each morning. One day, Shahrazad asked her father to put her name forward as the next bride. Her father tried to talk her out of this dangerous course. She told him that she had learned all her lessons well. "Trust me," she told her father. Her father eventually did as she asked. The King and Shahrazad married.

In the morning, she asked her husband for one last favor. Could she tell her sister a story? He agreed. And she told the story, and it was night again. So he spared her life that night. And she told another story and another. Each night for one thousand and one nights, Shahrazad told a story that saved her life, until the King finally decided she had told enough stories and he allowed her to live. That's how we got *Alf Layla wa-Layla, A Thousand Nights and One Night*. Even though Baba says Shahrazad was not a historical person, I believe someone like her existed. Maybe many someones like her.

When Baba first told me this tale, I said, "A King can kill people?"

Baba said, "A King can do anything. But he has someone he must answer to—even if it is his own conscience. Everyone has someone like the King in their lives. Shahrazad was clever. She didn't wait for her fate. She went to the King and said, 'Let me tell you a story.'

And she saved her own life. No sense crying and wailing over how terrible your life is. Someone always has it worse. Someone always has it better."

Before you went to sleep tonight, Umar, you said, "I want to see the moon."

"But we have no window," I said.

You gently pulled my scarf away until you could see my scar. I leaned down, and you kissed it. I will never have a husband, and I will probably always be a servant in a household like this one, but I have the best brother in the world. Your breath on my cheek—on my scar—felt like the breath of Allah.

You said, "Promise you will never leave me."

"I promise," I said. "Promise you will never leave me."

"Never," you said.

Good night, sweet brother. Dream of the two of us flying on a magic carpet, will you? We are flying far far from here.

Your loving sister, Nadira

May 31

SOMEDAY I WILL BRING YOU TO THIS place where I work, Umar. It is so big, and Begum Naseem and her husband, Tariq Saleem, and their children don't seem to notice how big it is. At first I sometimes got lost, but after three years I know it well. Do you remember when I came here to work? It was two years before Baba died. We needed the income, and our parents became certain then of what I already knew: They would not find a husband for me.

Umar, you would hardly believe all that the three children here are blessed with. They have their own rooms, each with a bathroom, television set, and telephone. The boy has a computer. I'm not sure exactly what it does, but I often hear his mother complain, "Duri spends too much time on that computer. What does he see on that screen?" I have stood looking at the screen, which is like a television, and I have seen nothing. When Duri just touches it, the screen brightens. I have tried that when he is not at home, but it remains dark.

They are very proud of their son, naturally, and his two sisters spoil him. The eldest, Noor, is getting married soon. We are already preparing for the wedding feasts. Today I helped Cook. They call her Cook, as though she has no name, but when I asked her what her name was, she frowned and said, "Cook." So I call her that too. She has lived with this family a long while.

Did Baba ever tell you his father worked here before he came to live with us? Our grandfather was Begum Naseem's gardener. She says he was very good.

"He talked to the plants and the earth," Begum Naseem told me. "Sometimes he even argued with them." She laughed. "And the gardens were always beautiful. He lived in that tiny house in back."

"The one where all the garden tools are now?" I asked.

"Yes, but he had it fixed up nicely. He'd have tea out

there. Plus his bed and some books. Your grandmother had died many years before. Then he retired and went to live with you. Do you remember him?"

"Yes," I told her. "He lived only a few years after he moved in with us. He was always trying to teach me and my mother the names of flowers. We weren't very good at remembering them. My father used to say I had a way with animals just like my grandfather had a way with plants."

I did not tell her that my skill was not much use any longer, since I never really encounter animals here, except the dead ones in the market. We owned a cow when we lived in the village. She liked me. Sometimes when I walked alone in the hills, the wild animals did not run away from me. I wonder if that would still be true?

But never mind about all that. I was saying I worked with Cook today. More and more I have been helping Cook with the meals. I like cooking much better than cleaning. I can smell the jasmine flowers from outside the kitchen window while I am rinsing the lentils for dal. I close my eyes and breathe deeply and imagine twining the flowers together to wear as a necklace I can smell all day long! I put seeds on the windowsill and sometimes a small bird or two will fly in and take them.

Cook often says something like, "Pay attention to your work! Quickly! Pick the stones out of the lentils."

Cook is very old. She worked in the household of Begum Naseem's mother's mother! She remembers when Begum Naseem's mother was born. She talks to herself all the time, and lately she says she is going to live with her granddaughter out in the country.

We made tea for Begum Naseem's friends this afternoon. They were awaiting the arrival of the choori woman. I was looking forward to seeing all the beautiful bangles. It was the birthday of one of the women, so Begum Naseem asked the choori wali to bring extra bangles.

While Cook sat and drank tea and rested her "old wrinkled soles," I made samosas and pakoras. I do not want to be disrespectful, but Ami is a much better cook than Cook. When Baba had the store in the village, Ami used to prepare delicious meals. No one could make pulao like she could. She knew exactly when to buy produce so that it tasted fresh off the vine or out of the ground. And her biryani! It is still good, as you know, but it used to be so much better when we lived in the village.

Cook's samosas and pakoras are too spicy; when she told me how much chili powder to put in, I sprinkled in less. Her halwa is too sweet. Ami says, "Too much hot and too much sweet is the disguise of a bad cook." Not that Cook is bad. She is just tired. She let me make the masala chai all by myself because she knows Begum Naseem likes the way I prepare it. All the women like my masala chai so much that I am usually allowed to sit off to the side while the choori wali shows her goods.

Our mother and father differed slightly on how to brew masala chai. Baba liked to boil it. Ami thought boiling bruised the essence of the tea.

Ami showed me her way; I remember it well because she repeated the steps and the story many times.

As she put a pot of water over the heat for chai, she said, "Masala chai has been with us for thousands of years. They say the King protected the recipe as one of his most cherished treasures. This was because it had magical and medicinal properties."

She crushed a couple of cardamom pods, whole cloves, and a cinnamon stick and dropped them into the water, along with black tea leaves. The concoction simmered for a bit. Then our mother poured it all into the teakettle and let it steep. "The King's servants prepared buckets and buckets of masala chai for his subjects every day. He was a good king, you see. His people were renowned for their good health and longevity."

Then Ami put fresh whole milk into the teakettle along with some sugar or honey. She poured the whole concoction back into the pan, then into the teakettle again. After a moment she poured it from the kettle into waiting cups. "I have heard it said that the first masala chai made from the original recipe could cure any ailment and would help you live a long and healthy life," she said. The recipe was eventually stolen from the King. What the thieves didn't know was that the King had changed the recipe just slightly, so their masala chai was not the real masala chai. To this day, that is why nearly everyone changes the recipe they know a bit—they are trying to brew the King's original masala

chai. Maybe someday you will figure it out, daughter."
And then she handed me a cup of masala chai.

Umar, someday Ami and I will teach you how to
prepare masala chai. Today I served Begum Naseem,
Noor, and their friends masala chai, samosas, pakoras,
and halwa.

"I love your tea, Nadira," Noor said. "It's always just
the right blend of milk and sweetener."

"And these samosas! Usually I can't eat samosas
because they are so hot," another woman said. "Yours
are wonderful!"

I was glad Cook was not in the room to hear these
praises. She might have thought they were veiled criti-
cisms of her cooking. The bangle woman came in
soon after. You would have been amazed at her baskets
of bangles. I have never seen so many different colors!
The women kept slipping (or pushing) on bangle after
bangle: orange, blue, maroon, red, purple, gold. Noor
danced around the room with her arms covered in
bangles, her hair laced with jasmine.

"I have such big hands," one of the women said.
Each woman always wants to be the one who can wear

the smallest bangle, which would mean they have the smallest hands.

"Oh, why do you bring us such small bangles?" Begum Naseem asked. "We are old women with fat hands."

"She is not speaking for me!" one of the women said, snatching the tiny bangle and trying to push her hand through it. She could not, so Noor tried. She failed too. Then the next woman and the next one.

"I know who can wear it," Noor said, running over to me. Before I could stop her, she slipped the bangle up over my hand. "Just like a baby's hand," she said, holding my fingers in hers for a moment. "She is the tiniest of us all. I envy your hands, Nadira. There, keep the bangle. It looks good on you."

I smiled. Out of the corner of my vision, I saw Begum Naseem shaking her head at Noor. I quickly slipped off the gold bangle and gave it back to her. I pulled my scarf closer to my face, and then I picked up the nearly empty halwa tray as an excuse to leave the room.

"Noor," I heard her mother say as I walked down the hall, "how can you be so insensitive?"

"I was just showing everyone how beautiful and tiny her hands are," Noor said.

I went to the empty kitchen and put more halwa on the plate. I could not wear one bangle. No one wore one bangle. But even two arms covered in bangles would not hide the scar on my face—even though my dupatta did a good job of it. I walked to the sink, turned on the water, and washed my hands.

Our mother's bangles were the one thing we had not sold when we moved to Karachi. After our father died, Ami took off all her bangles, as widows often do, and she smashed them. She broke each and every one into pieces. "There, my life is over," she said. "Now everyone knows it."

I took a deep breath and went back into the room full of women. I put the plate of halwa on the table and then sat back on the floor away from them.

"Did you hear they rescued four more children who had been used as camel kids?" one woman asked as she pushed on several bangles and then shook them off again.

"Did they steal the children or did their parents sell them?" Begum Naseem asked.

"What kind of parents would sell their children to ride camels for some Sheikh?" Noor asked.

"A very poor parent," Begum Naseem answered. "Poverty is a stick some parents cannot spare their children."

"Three of these children didn't even know their real names," the woman said, "or who their parents are. What their language was. They all had had broken bones. All four were under the age of ten and had been working as camel riders for years."

Noor shook her head. "The things people do for entertainment."

June 5

TOMORROW I GET TO SEE YOU, little brother! I will feel your tiny fingers wrapped around my fingers. Don't worry, Umar. Someday you will be bigger than I am. You will be teasing me about how small I am. Sometimes I wish I were bigger—or at least looked older. People still see me as a child even though I am eighteen years old.

Yesterday I was cleaning the library here when I saw *Alf Layla wa-Layla* on the shelf. I carefully brought it out, put it on the table, and opened it up. Begum Naseem came in while I was looking at it. I thought she would be mad, but she wasn't.

"You can take that to your room and read it at night

if you like," she said. "If you promise to be careful."

"Thank you," I said. "Seeing it reminded me of my father. He used to read from a copy his mother had given him when he was a boy. She could read and write, too. She wrote in it, 'To my beloved son. Remember Shahrazad, and always learn wisely.'"

Begum Naseem nodded. "I never had the pleasure of meeting your grandmother. Do you read from your father's copy now that he is gone?"

"No, he sold it along with most of our belongings when we moved here," I said. "So he could get goods for his stall at the market. He sold rice and beans."

"Yes, I remember," Begum Naseem said.

I keep forgetting she knew our father.

"How is your mother?"

I didn't know how to answer that question. So I told the truth.

"She is worried about expenses," I said. "I give her everything."

"But your brothers?"

I could feel the red rising to my face.

"Perhaps they do not know," she said.

"I have written several times," I said. "My oldest brother works in an oil field and no women are allowed, so my mother cannot live with him there, and his wife and children are already crowded back in Islamabad. My mother says they have their own lives."

"But it is their responsibility," she said.

"After we left the village," I said, "it all changed." I touched my cheek. I couldn't help it. I wish I could stop that particular habit. I will have to work on it. I don't think Begum Naseem noticed.

"Is your mother working?"

"Not since my father died," I said. "She was cooking and cleaning for a woman, but that lady died shortly before my father did."

"Well, give your mother my regards," Begum Naseem said. "Let me know if she needs anything."

"She is grateful that you let me work and stay here," I said.

"We're glad to have you," Begum Naseem said. "I appreciate your help."

I could tell she was uncomfortable and wanted to leave, so I started to put the book back on the shelf.

"Why don't you keep it?" she said. "My children never use this library."

"Thank you," I said.

She nodded and left me alone. I slipped the book back into its place on the shelf. I did not want to be ungrateful, but I did not want her copy. I wanted Baba's. Inside that copy was true magic. At least I believed that at one time. Now I was not certain about anything.

I finished cleaning the room and counted the hours until I saw you and Ami.

June 8

DEAREST BROTHER, YOU KNOW by now I was not able to come home. Cook fell and hurt herself and had to go to the hospital. I had to stay and help Begum Naseem. She is a good cook too, but she gets nervous, especially when other people come into the kitchen.

"I did this—cook—when I was first married," Begum Naseem told me. "I can do it now."

That lasted twenty-four hours. Then she hired a temporary replacement for Cook, although I don't think Cook will be coming back. Her granddaughter has arrived from the country and wants to take her home with her.

I sometimes miss living in the country. We knew everyone in the village; they knew us. It is not like that here. Ami trusts no one in the city. Too many thieves, she told me when we first came here. I said to her, "Maybe we'll be like Ali Baba, and we'll find the treasure of the forty thieves!"

"Open sesame!" Baba said.

"You've given this girl too many ideas," Ami said. "What is she going to do with them all?"

Baba laughed and said, "If she has too many ideas, perhaps she can sell some of them. Open a shop of ideas. What do you say, daughter of mine?"

Baba was in good spirits that day. He had just started selling his beans and rice.

"She could call it 'One thousand ideas and one idea.'"

Ami had to laugh too. You were so tiny then, just a baby, and the scar on my face had barely healed. You were such a gift to our family, Umar. We had such a celebration after you were born. After I was hurt, I would sometimes pretend you were my own child, because I knew I would never have one of my own. How could I? No man would marry me. But even before, Umar, know that we all cherished you.

In the village, few girls could read. Baba taught me to read and write; he even taught me English, in case we went to England someday, he said. Before I was hurt, some of the women warned our mother that no man would want to marry me because I would think I was better than a man who could not read. She didn't tell them she could read too.

That was before our eldest brother was accused. Rahman swears he never touched that girl. He admitted he hoped Baba and Ami could arrange a marriage between them, but he never followed her out to the patch of bluebells, as they claimed. I wonder what the girl said. I have forgotten her name. Isn't that strange? Did *she* accuse Rahman? I think it was her brothers and father. They were jealous of Baba. He was smarter and richer. They owed him money. Baba knew they were poor, so he gave them credit. Maybe he would not let them get anything else until they paid off their debt. I do not really know. They went to the elders and the other men of the village and accused Rahman. Without Baba being there. He was found guilty and the sentence

was . . . Can I actually write it here? Will I be con-
demned if I do? Will my scar suddenly burst into
flames and burn my skin? Will someone find out I
spoke of it and come in the night and pour acid on me
or you and Ami? They did that to my friend Ausha
when her parents refused a proposal of marriage for
her. It was terrible, Umar. They poured acid on the
whole family while they slept. Her little brother was
killed. She was disfigured. I would never do anything
to hurt you, dear brother. Not that Ausha did anything either.

I should stop thinking about this. Fatima is home
with her family, so she cannot hear my weeping or see
my tears. The sentence they handed out for our brother's alleged crime was that the father and brothers of
the girl got permission to attack Rahman's sister: me.

And so they did. That is how I got the scar.

Perhaps I have told you too much, little brother.

When we moved to Karachi, I overheard Ami talking to Auntie Parveen.

"What did you expect? That girl Rahman had his

eye on became damaged property. So they had to damage his father's property: your daughter."

"But none of it was true," Ami said. "Rahman did nothing to the girl."

Auntie Parveen shrugged and said, "We are nothing in this world. Now Nadira is less than nothing. At least she won't have the burden of marriage and motherhood."

"You would rather she lived in servitude and poverty?"

"What is the difference between her life and ours?" Auntie Parveen asked. "I was given to this man Rubel—your brother, I know—and must do his bidding until he dies. That was not my choice. Getting ruined by those men was not Nadira's choice. So what?"

"She was not ruined," Ami said. "She got away from them before they could rape her. That's why they scarred her face."

"So she says," Auntie Parveen said. "But they did touch her. That is enough. And she is soiled."

Ami's anger melted then, and she wept. Auntie Parveen hesitated, and then she put her arm around our mother. She is not so mean as she pretends. She has a hard life. Anyone who lives with Uncle Rubel has a difficult life.

I sometimes think maybe Rahman doesn't come home and help our mother because he feels shame over what happened in the village. Even if he never touched that girl—and I believe he did not—I must be a constant reminder to him of what happened. Me and my scarred face.

But back to Cook getting hurt. They hired a new cook. Did I say that? She is not a kind woman. We had a lull in activity after we cleaned up after lunch, so I was feeding the birds on the windowsill. A finch actually took seeds from my hand, just like birds used to in the village. The new cook walked over and slapped my hand.

"Get back to work!" she said.

Begum Naseem walked by just then.

"We do not hit people in this house," Begum Naseem said.

"She was feeding a wild bird!" the woman exclaimed. "What about the bird flu?"

Begum Naseem sighed. She does not like confrontation—who does? "I will prepare dinner. You may go home for the day."

The woman made a noise, then left the room. I do not know why, Umar, but I thought this was all very funny. I had to put my hand over my mouth to keep from laughing. Begum Naseem starting laughing too.

"I should have sneezed," Begum Naseem said.

"And I could have coughed," I said.

I could not believe I said that out loud! But she laughed, and then we cooked dinner together.

"Did your mother teach you to cook?" Begum Naseem asked while we prepared the chicken curry. (I did the chicken. She made kheer—it is difficult for anyone to make bad rice pudding, after all!)

I told her Ami had taught me all I knew and that Cook had tried to unteach me. For some reason, Begum Naseem laughs at the things I say—the kinds of things Ami says I should keep to myself. Begum Naseem reminds me of Baba in that way, but I need to be careful. She is my employer and I am her servant.

She is kind, though, and kindness is a great gift to bestow on anyone, Umar.

"I have an idea, Nadira," Begum Naseem said. "Would your mother be interested in helping out during the wedding? Cooking, I mean. Then if that works out, she and your brother could move into the little house your grandfather used to live in. I could have Saliq clean it out and make some alterations. There might be room to add a small bathroom and half-kitchen."

I was so excited I could barely keep from jumping up and down. You and Ami would have a good place to live, and we would see one another all the time. I pretended I was very calm, however, Umar. I said, "I will ask Ami when I go home. This is very kind, Begum Naseem."

Afterward, I went and looked at the tiny house. It is not truly a house. It is almost like a dollhouse! But you and Ami are small people, and it is bigger than the rooms you now live in. Saliq was working nearby, on the gardens. He is a young unmarried man who has taken over a gardening business from his father. He has helped his father, Haji Abdul Razzak, for many years, but not many words have passed between us. I have seen friends of Begum Naseem's daughters flirt with him, and he does not respond. He may be a traditionalist, like the men in the village. Perhaps he is just shy. Or maybe he understands his place. If he responded to the girls, he would probably be fired. Of course, as soon as they see him limping, they lose interest in him.

Saliq does not work as quickly as his father did—because of the limp—but I think he does a better job. He handles the flowers gently, and I have never seen him yank anything out of the ground, the way his father sometimes did. He does not work here full-time, of course, since there isn't enough work. He also takes care of a few other houses on the street. He nods when he sees me and smiles slightly, without actually looking at me. I only mention his work because I believe he will do a good job on the tiny house. He is a careful worker.

I miss you and our mother so much, little brother! I will be so glad if you can come here to live. Maybe we have unknowingly said the secret words—like "sesame"—to open the doors to the treasures of life!

See you soon.

June 10

TODAY BEGUM NASEEM CAME and told me that I was needed at home, immediately. She even had Saliq drive me there. I knew something was wrong when I got into the truck and no one else was there. It doesn't matter since I am already ruined.

As we drove away from Begum Naseem and Tariq Saleem's house and got closer to our neighborhood, I noticed how quickly the color seemed to drain out of the city. I thought of Baba's stall at the market. When he first opened it, it was so colorful and tidy. Not a grease stain on anything. The top of the stall was covered in red. Oh, the brightness of that red! Everyone knew my father had the finest beans, the best rice. But it didn't matter. Soon his stall looked like all the other stalls.

"I am selling goods to poor people," he said, "so I will always be poor."

"But, Baba," I said. "Didn't you sell to poor people in the village, too?"

He didn't answer. He stared away from me. Baba lost hope, Umar. That was what happened. He hated this place. I heard him tell Ami that if he could get a place in the Empress Market then maybe things would be better. He had had a place there once, before I was born, but our second brother Hasan had asthma and the doctor told Baba and Ami they needed to get away from the city. So they moved to the village.

Poor Baba. Do you think he felt ruined by his children? He did everything for us. Left the city for Hasan, left the country for me—and Rahman. It was not my fault what happened. Or Rahman's.

I am glad Baba was not alive to find what I found when Saliq drove me to that shack Uncle Rubel makes us call home. Ami was there, crying, along with Auntie Parveen. Uncle Rubel paced the tiny room.

"Ami, Ami," I said, dropping onto my knees in front of her. "What has happened? Where is Umar?"

"He is gone!" Ami cried. "We have searched for him for two days."

"Two days! Why didn't someone come and get me? I know Umar's hiding places. Have you searched the market? He sometimes likes to go to Baba's old stall. Or his friend Almas?"

"He was playing with Almas when it happened," Auntie Parveen said.

"Can I get any tea around here?" Uncle Rubel said.

Our mother started to get up. I hung on to her legs, so Auntie Parveen fetched Uncle Rubel his tea instead. He was sweating more than usual, and I wondered if he was sick. But I didn't care, brother. I only wanted to know where you were.

"Please, what happened?" I asked.

"The smugglers got him," Uncle Rubel said.

"What smugglers? Ami, what is he talking about?"

Uncle Rubel gave me a dirty look. I pulled my scarf closer, down over my scar.

"They were here last week," Auntie Parveen said.

"They asked Rubel if they could have Umar to train as a camel kid," Ami said.

"Of course I said it was outrageous," Uncle Rubel said, "but I asked your mother, out of respect. It has been very difficult since your father died. It is only out of the goodness of my heart that you, your mother, and brother still have a home here. You are family, of course, and I promised our dear parents I would always look after my only sister, but I have debts to pay, too, and I could get a good sum for this place."

I wanted to shout that we didn't need his hovel any longer—now that Begum Naseem had offered us a place to live—but I held my tongue.

"Almas described the men who took Umar," Auntie Parveen said, "and they were the same smugglers who approached Rubel. They tried to get Almas, too, but he ran faster. Umar has always been a little slow."

"He is just small!" I snapped. "Did you go to the police?"

"Yes, your uncle took me," Ami said. "They said they

would go to the docks and search the ships and go to the airport and search the airplanes, but I don't know if they will."

"I'll go look for him," I said. "I know him better than anyone else."

"I have already looked," Uncle Rubel said.

"Could one of my cousins come with me so I can look for Umar?" I asked. We never see them, I know, because they think they are better than we are, but I thought maybe now when we were so desperate they would actually help. But Uncle Rubel said his sons were all busy. Then he took Auntie Parveen away for their dinner.

I wish I could describe to you what that night was like, Umar. I know you will want to know when you are safely home again. But it is difficult. Everything felt blurry, out of focus, like when we first moved here. Nothing seemed solid. It was the worst night of my life, little brother. Ami and I could not eat. We both sat silently on the floor, a dish of biryani before us. I could not sleep. I kept thinking of you screaming as the smugglers carried you away. Only Almas said you did not scream. He said they whispered something in your ear, and you reached your hand up and went with them. What was it they said, Umar? How did they get you to so easily leave your family? Oh, my boy, I hope they are treating you well. They would want you healthy, wouldn't they? To ride their precious camels? I must hold on to that thought.

June 11

C I AWAKENED THIS MORNING
and turned over expecting you to be on your rug, but
you were not. It was almost more than I could bear.
Poor Ami. She was so distraught her hands shook.

We decided to ignore Uncle Rubel, and we went out
looking for you ourselves. We went to many, many mar-
kets. We even traveled all the way to the Empress
Market to see if you somehow found your way there. So
many young boys wandering the streets. I kept thinking, "Why didn't they take one of them?" Isn't that terrible? They should not be taking anyone. We went to
the police again. I did not like it there, Umar, and hope
we do not have to return. It was so noisy! It smelled

worse than Uncle Rubel. The constable kept getting interrupted. He said they were doing all they could. Many people had reported stolen children, he said, and the police would work very hard to find them only to discover later that the family had actually sold the children. Which was illegal, too, the constable warned. He treated us like we were criminals.

The city seems too big, Umar. Where are you?

June 13

WE CRY OURSELVES TO SLEEP, Ami and I. It is too sad in this place. Tomorrow I will have to return to work. I want to take Mother with me, but she believes you will return here. I told her Auntie Parveen will make certain you know where we are.

I am sorry to tell you, Umar, but the body of a young boy was returned to his parents today. He lived down the street. He was only two years older than you. His parents sold him to the smugglers, and now they only have his lifeless body. I thought Ami would collapse right there and then when she heard the boy's mother screaming.

June 14

I WENT TO WORK TODAY, UMAR. I dreamed you were crying and calling for me. I want to keep looking for you but cannot go on my own. It is times like these when I wish I were a man—or a boy—so I could look for you by myself more freely. I keep crying. I cannot help it. And you know that is unusual. I don't cry. I am afraid you are dead. But wouldn't I feel it? Wouldn't I know that my baby brother was dead? I didn't know when Baba died. I was at work. I knew he was sick, of course, but I didn't know that he would close his eyes and never open them again on that particular day. I was laughing and cleaning the house with Fatima. I remember. And Baba was gone.

I do not want to think about these things.

Saliq cleaned out the tiny house. He painted it too, and workers are coming in to put in the tiny kitchen and tiny bathroom. Duri saw it and told his mother that he wanted to live there. I was so afraid they would let him. Then where would Ami be? At least if she is here I can look after her. I hope she will recover enough from your disappearance to be able to cook for Begum Naseem and her family. If I knew where the smugglers took the camel kids, maybe I could get someone to go there and rescue you. I don't know what to do.

June 16

AS EACH DAY GOES BY WITHOUT
news of you, I am more and more frightened. Begum
Naseem is very understanding, but I must not lose this
job or we will all be out in the street. I went home to
get Ami today. Saliq drove me. Duri came with us, sitting in the middle. Uncle Rubel was with Ami, along
with Auntie Parveen. He wore a new tunic, and Auntie
Parveen was up to her elbows in new bangles. They
both sparkled. Saliq put Ami's things in the back of the
truck, along with what we had left of Baba's. I held on
to the bag containing your clothes and few toys—and
your little book from Baba: "Learn wisely."

I asked Baba once what his mother meant by signing

his copy of *Alf Layla wa-Layla*, "Learn wisely." And he asked me what I thought it meant.

"You should try not to learn stupid things," I said.

He laughed. "Perhaps. But how does one manage to learn only wise things?"

"I guess we just have to keep learning," I said, "so that you can figure out what is wise knowledge and what is unwise."

"Very good, daughter," he said. "I have wondered for forty years what she meant, and now I know."

As I clutched your bag to myself, Umar, I realized I must learn wisely now. I knew that Uncle Rubel would not help us. The police didn't seem to know anything. I wrote to our brothers, but I had not heard back from them. The smugglers had kidnapped other children. I had to find someone who could help me.

The work was not completed on the tiny house, so Ami slept with me and Fatima.

Before we went to sleep, I whispered to Ami, "Did you notice Uncle Rubel's new tunic and Auntie Parveen's bangles?"

"Yes," she said. "What of it?"

"Where did they get the money?" I asked. "Is it possible Rubel sold Umar to the smugglers?"

"My own brother?" She was silent for a moment. Then she said, "Yes, it is possible. He was a mean boy when he was a child. He has become a mean man."

"We must go to the police and tell them," I said.

"No, he would hurt us if he found out," Ami said. "We must find another way. Perhaps if I tell him it is all right—pretend it is all right—then he will give me the names of the men, and we can turn over the names to the police."

"Do you think he would tell you?" I asked.

"I will do my best," Ami said.

"That has always been good enough," I said.

June 19

AS AMI AND I WERE BRINGING
her things into the tiny house, Saliq came by with his
father, Haji Abdul Razzak.

"Bibi Mariam," Haji Abdul Razzak said, speaking to
Ami, "we were sorry to hear about your son."

Ami did not look at Saliq's father. I glanced at Saliq
when I knew he was watching his father. His fingers
moved nervously over the mala beads wrapped around
his wrist.

"My nephew was kidnapped by smugglers three
years ago," Haji Abdul Razzak said.

"Did he come home?"

Haji Abdul Razzak looked down at his feet, then glanced at his son.

"No, he has not come home," he answered, "but we went to a man who has had some success in getting other children returned."

"Who is this man?" our mother asked.

"His name is Mr. Bashir. He spends part of his time here and part on the peninsula tracking down kidnapped children."

"Would he come see us?" Ami asked.

"I could go to his office and inquire," Saliq said, "on my day off."

"That would be very kind," Ami said.

Our mother and I went to see Uncle Rubel again. Auntie Parveen made us tea and even served samosas. They were greasy and had no flavor. The masala chai tasted like water. Auntie Parveen did not wear the new bangles.

"I have decided what happened to Umar is the best thing," Ami said.

"What could you mean?" Auntie Parveen asked, sounding horrified. I say she *sounded* horrified because she looked more frightened than anything else. Uncle Rubel pretended he was interested in none of it and kept twirling the ring on his little finger.

"I have heard they pay the families of the camel kids," Ami said. "It's a way for Umar to contribute to his family. Then after a few years he can come home."

Our mother lied very convincingly. Uncle Rubel gulped his masala chai too fast, and he started coughing.

"Woman! This tea tastes like camel dung!"

If I hadn't been so worried about you, Umar, I would have laughed.

"Brother, if you know who those men were," Ami said, "if you can tell me where they are, I wish you would. I would like to see my son once before he leaves."

"What nonsense this is, sister!" Uncle Rubel said. "I don't know these men. If I did, they could not take you to your son because he would be gone already, set down somewhere in the desert."

"What country?" By now Ami was having difficulty not crying.

"He could be where the Sheikhs race," Uncle Rubel said. "Or somewhere else. How am I to know?"

Our mother pushed herself up off the floor and stood over her younger brother.

"You would know because you sold my son to these wicked people! If you do not tell me where those men are, then you are no longer my brother. And may Allah's messengers curse you from this moment on. May they hunt you down and make your life as miserable as you have made my son's!"

Aunt Parveen gasped. Uncle Rubel jumped to his feet and raised his hand to hit Ami. I was quicker. I stepped between them and pulled my mother away.

We hurried outside.

"Beware your actions, Mariam!" We could hear him shouting.

Saliq stood beside the truck, waiting. When he saw us, he opened the passenger door, but our mother got in the back of the truck, with the gardening equipment.

"Ami!" I said. "What are you doing? It is going to rain any moment."

"Bibi Mariam, please," Saliq said. "I cannot leave you out in the rain."

You know our mother, Umar. For some reason, she had decided to be in the back of the truck, so in the back of the pickup she would be. I think she wanted to humiliate Uncle Rubel by humiliating herself.

Finally I got in the back with her.

"It is all right," I said to Saliq. "Go ahead."

Saliq reluctantly got into the truck and drove us away from Rubel's house. Our scarves did not keep off the rain, which started almost immediately. We were drenched by the time we got home.

Begum Naseem was angry with Saliq. I could hear her chastising him as Fatima led me and Ami back to our room to change clothes.

"She is a widow! You left her out in the rain and cold! This is unacceptable!"

I imagined Saliq looking at his feet.

"To treat these women as though they are nothing, as though they are garbage to be thrown in the back of the truck!"

"Saliq, you may go," I heard Begum Naseem's husband Tariq Saleem say.

I will admit to you, Umar, I hung back so I could listen.

"My wife, Bibi Mariam told you she insisted on riding in the back. They are wet; they are not harmed. Come, this is just stress from the wedding."

Then their words became muffled, and I started shivering so I hurried back to change.

Poor Saliq. Still, I envy his freedom. If I were Saliq, I could go see Mr. Bashir myself. I had heard Begum Naseem and Noor talking earlier about two women who had acid thrown at them by traditionalists as they were walking down the street alone. It is not that I am afraid to go out in the world and risk it for you, Umar. It is only that if something happens to me, no one will be left to fight for you.

June 20

THIS HOUSE IS GIDDY, UMAR, because of the upcoming wedding. The house itself, yes! Like something magical from Sindbad's journey. I half expect to step onto a carpet and be whisked away from here. I long for that—if it would take me to your side. Do you remember the tale of "Prince Ahmed and Periebanou?" It's the one where the princes are looking for extraordinary treasures to impress their father so he will let one of them wed Princess Nouronnihar. Prince Houssain found a carpet that would take him any place he wished: instantly. I would come to you, brother, and bring you back home.

Home. What a strange idea. Where is our home?

Perhaps Ami was right about our father teaching me too many things. Did I learn wisely? I feel so bound up here. As though I cannot breathe. Or move. I feel helpless to find you. I want to scream. Why aren't they all doing something more to rescue you?

Begum Naseem feels bad about scolding Saliq, I think. She had me take him out cold tea and samosas mid-afternoon while he was helping to put flowers up all around the property. Tariq Saleem keeps changing his mind about where he wants everything for the wedding.

I took the tea out to Saliq.

"Shukria," he said.

"You are welcome," I replied, and started to walk away.

"I hope you and your mother are both well," he said.

I stopped. "Yes, we are fine."

"You didn't catch a cold?" he asked. "I didn't want to leave you in the back of the truck."

"My mother is having a very difficult time because my brother is gone," I said. "I am certain she is sorry you were scolded because of our actions."

Then I walked back to the house. Mayoun, the yellow

day, is soon upon us. I will not have time to do anything but cook, cook, and cook. We sleep in the tiny house now. Sometimes I go outside and look at the stars. One night I saw a falling star, and I remembered a story Baba told me when I was a little girl and we still lived in the village. We could see so many stars then, Umar. The sky was crowded with them! One night a star flashed across the sky, leaving behind a fading path of light.

"Baba!" I cried. "What was that?"

"A falling star," he said. "If you look around you might find it."

"Truly?" I glanced at the ground. "What would it look like?"

Baba laughed. "It would look just like you!" he said. "Fallen stars are children who have lost their way. They are children who wandered too far from their parents and ended up in the sky. Of course, they cannot stay up there forever, so eventually they fall back down to the Earth. If they are lucky, they find their parents again. If not, they end up as those shiny bits you see in the sand."

My mouth opened wide. I looked up at the multitude of stars. "All of those are lost children?" I whispered.

"No, just the falling stars," he said. "But don't worry. You will never wander that far from your baba and ami, will you?"

I shook my head.

"Then you are safe, my daughter."

Baba took my hand, and we started for home. I glanced up at the sky and wondered if it might be nice to be a star, even a fallen one, for just a little while. I looked up at Baba, and he smiled at me, and I decided I could not risk being separated from our parents forever. I would remain happily Earthbound.

June 21

BEGUM NASEEM HAD ME CLEAN out the children's closets. I do this a couple times a year, usually when Begum Naseem feels the children have been acting spoiled and selfish. I am not certain what precipitated her request this time. Noor has been crying a great deal, and the father has had a headache. Noor knows the man she is marrying. She even *wants* to marry him! That must make it easier. I am glad I will never be forced to marry someone like Rubel. We have so much to do in the house to prepare for the wedding feasts, so I was surprised Begum Naseem wanted me to clean closets. But I did it.

The children looked through what I picked out and

did not put anything back. I stuffed the clothes into bags that I set out back to be taken to the poverty center later. Begum Naseem told me I could have whatever I wanted, so I took some of Duri's clothes for when you get bigger, two saris for Ami, and a couple of scarves for me. It was quite a treasure, Umar. You will be excited to see it all even if it will be years before you fit into them.

Saliq and his father came to tell us Mr. Bashir would visit the house tomorrow morning. Ami asked the men if they would like some masala chai. When they said yes, she served them as we sat on a mat on the ground outside the tiny house. It was a warm night that smelled of jasmine and cinnamon. The big house was all lit up. We could hear Noor and her sister and mother laughing. Every once in a while, we heard Tariq Saleem's laughter too.

"I am sorry there is not more to tell you about our visit with Bashir," Haji said. "Our meeting was brief. We gave him the description of Umar you gave us. And we told him about your brother Rubel and where he lives. Bashir says before he comes here tomorrow he will visit

Rubel. Mr. Bashir rescued several boys last month."

"We are very grateful for your help," Ami said.

"My father, this is very good masala chai," Saliq said.

His father nodded. "Indeed it is."

"My mother knows how to buy the freshest spices," I said. "She grinds them carefully, delicately, until they turn to dust out of love for her."

Haji smiled. Our mother did not even scold me. She and I are both outcasts now, widow and wounded daughter, so we are freer, in some ways, than other people. There is not much more they could take from us, is there? Now that you are gone, brother.

"My dear late wife made good tea too," Haji said. "It is a useful skill to have."

I could tell Saliq's father liked our mother. He is no match for Baba—except he is here and Baba is dead. He seemed a kind man, but I wondered if he could read and write. Did he know any of the stories of the Arabian nights? I could not think of a subtle way to ascertain this.

Our mother said, "My daughter fancies herself Shahrazad, but she is also a good cook."

"Oh?" Haji said. "And who is your king?"

I was glad it was dark because I could feel my face burn with embarrassment. I had known this man for many years. I was certain he knew about my scar.

"I do not care about the King," I said. "It is Shahrazad herself who holds my interest. The King killed his wives, one after another, because he had been betrayed by one woman. He could not stand to be hurt again, so he would take a wife for one night, then kill her. That was extreme. We all are hurt again and again. He was a king. He should have known better, but he was only concerned about himself. Shahrazad wanted to save her community from this man. So she offered herself—not as a sacrifice. She knew she had the ability to save herself and the rest of the women in her community. She knew she could do that."

"By telling a good story," Saliq said.

"Yes, exactly," I said. "Do you know *Alf Layla wa-Layla*?"

"Saliq went to school," his father said.

"One of my teachers read to us from *A Thousand Nights and One Night*," Saliq said.

"You are fortunate," Ami said. "My older boys went

to school for a time, but neither Nadira or Umar went."

"Baba was the best teacher," I said, "and Umar will come home and go to school."

"You have older sons?" Haji asked.

"I did," Ami said in such a way that we all knew the conversation was over.

The men took their leave, and Ami and I went back into the tiny house.

I was so excited about seeing Mr. Bashir!

"Maybe this man will find our Umar, Ami," I said. "We will be a family again."

"Saliq is a nice man," Ami said. "He is looking for a wife."

"Is he? What business is that of ours?"

Ami shrugged as she rinsed out the teacups.

"You think because I have a scar and he has a limp we should be satisfied with each other?" I asked.

"You would speak to your mother this way?" she asked.

I immediately felt ashamed, Umar. We had never argued before, but I did not want to think about Saliq—or anyone else—as my husband.

"I am sorry, Ami," I said. "I am just tired."

"Don't you ever desire marriage and a family?" she asked.

"I was very young when that possibility was taken away from me," I told her. "I barely had time to want it before it was gone."

"It is only a scar," Ami said. "You said nothing else happened."

"Even so," I said. "I dream of going to school. I dream of learning. I do not dream of marriage or children. My brother Umar is the only child I will ever have in my life."

"I am sorry," she said.

"Besides," I said, "if I marry, I would have to leave this place. It is so much better than where we lived. It is so much better than anything a gardener or anyone else could do for me."

Ami laughed. "I cannot argue with you about that," Ami said. "An unmarried woman just seems unnatural."

"Like a widow?" I said. "Perhaps it is time you remarried, then. Saliq's father is a widower."

She crinkled her nose. "He smells."

I laughed. "Like what? How did you get that close?"

"Like milk. Spoiled milk."

"He's probably been drinking masala chai with evap-
orated milk," I said. "You can just feed him better."

I couldn't sleep, brother. I had not been a good
daughter. I lied to my mother. I *have* thought of marriage and children. I am glad I am not forced to marry
someone like Rubel, but sometimes I imagine working
as a teacher with my husband and having children and
a nice house. In a different world. I would live near you
and Ami. You would have your family. We would be rich
enough so that Ami lived in comfort. She would never
again have to shiver on the floor of a hovel during a
cold rain because we could not afford to heat the stove.
She would have a beautiful silk sari in every color of
the rainbow. And bangles! Oh, Umar! Our house would
be surrounded with flowers and birds and beauty. Hope
is a terrible thing, isn't it?

I went outside and sat by the fish pond and cried. It
was the second time I had cried in recent days. I could
see the moon reflected in the pond. It was so bright.

And I thought of you touching my crescent moon scar. I even saw some stars in the water. Perhaps you were up in the sky and would fall to Earth any moment now, and I would find you in the grass somewhere. If only life were that simple.

"Are you all right?"

I looked up and saw Saliq standing over me. I wiped my eyes and glanced around. He was alone. My heart started racing.

He stepped back. "I apologize. I didn't mean to frighten you. I was walking to my truck and heard you crying."

"To your truck? What are you doing here so late?"

"Tariq Saleem had me take down the flowers in front of the house," Saliq said.

I could not help but laugh.

"He has gone quite mad with this wedding," I said.

"I studied in England for a few years," Saliq said.

I had no idea what that information had to do with anything.

"I got accustomed to how men and women are in England," he explained. "So I don't always know what is acceptable here. The distance between men and women now seems peculiar, yet I don't want to do anything that would jeopardize anyone."

"You lived here all your life and go away for a few years and you forget? You've been back for how many years?"

"Three years," he said. "I have a rich aunt who lives sometimes here and sometimes in England. She doesn't have any children, so she would take me back and forth with her. Anyway, I just mean I didn't intend to frighten you."

"I understand," I said. "I am an outcast, so to speak, so people don't pay attention to me. Your reputation could be ruined, however, if you are seen with me."

He sat across the pond from me.

"Well, you must have noticed my limp," he said. "I fell off a horse. In England. My father nearly went crazy when he found out. I am his only son. They operated, and it's much better. But my aunt lost interest in her crippled nephew."

"Even though she crippled you?"

"She didn't, actually. The horse did. But yes. I was

her handsome nephew until the accident, and then I became her crippled nephew and drew the wrong kind of attention to her."

"In England the men and women talk to each other freely, about these kinds of personal things?"

"Yes," he said. "They go out alone like this. They touch. They choose their own mates."

We were silent.

"Here, people are sometimes killed for such things."

Saliq shook his head and whispered, "Not here in this garden, near this house."

"Then I suppose I will tell you where I got the scar," I said. "It could have happened when I was on a voyage with Sindbad. Remember the seahorses? They would gallop onto shore and lovingly cover the mares waiting for them. But we would have to frighten them to get them to return to the ocean without the mares. Perhaps one of them kicked me."

I pulled my scarf away and turned my cheek to the moonlight.

"Yes," Saliq said, looking at the scar, "it could be the print of a seahorse's hoof."

"But wait," I said. "Have you not heard that a moon-shaped scar is the sign of the fairy queen, like the one who married Prince Amoud?"

"Ahhh, yes. She was very powerful and very clever. I see. The crescent moon scar—it is silver in the moonlight."

"Naturally," I said. "Someday, I will tell you the rest of the story—whether it is a fairy sign or a sea-horse sign."

He smiled. "I look forward to it."

"You are lucky you are not a woman," I said. "I am so frustrated because I can do nothing to help my brother. I wish I were a boy! I would go after him."

"How? I'm a man and I wouldn't know what to do. I didn't know what to do when my cousin disappeared."

"I don't know," I said, "but I would figure something out if I were a man."

"If you are all right," Saliq said, "I will go home now. My father gets worried."

"I did not need rescuing," I said, "but I thank you for your intended kindness. I won't tell anyone about it."

"Nor will I," he said.

And then he left me alone. I realized how silly it was to sit under the moon and cry. Somewhere you were sitting under the same moon, and I hoped you were not crying.

Someone will find you. Soon, brother, soon. I promise.

June 22

WE SAT IN THE ROOM WHERE I usually served tea, only this time I was on a chair and my mother sat on the sofa, and we all sipped masala chai while Mr. Bashir talked to Ami. Begum Naseem and her husband sat with us.

"Your brother Rubel was not very cooperative," Mr. Bashir said to Ami after everyone had been introduced and given tea. "He swore he had nothing to do with the kidnapping, but I was not convinced of his innocence, especially since he did tell me the names of the smugglers and gave me their descriptions. I know of them."

"What will happen to Umar?" Tariq Saleem asked.

"Most likely they will train him to ride the camels," he said. "They may or may not give him a helmet. He may or may not fall off. The truth is many of these children die or are badly injured. Those who survive are often turned out once they are too big to ride, and then they are picked up for being illegal immigrants and are put in jail. There they can stay indefinitely. The children who are rescued—and I have rescued many—often have been away from home so long that they don't remember who their parents are. They don't even remember their own language."

Ami started to cry. Begum Naseem put her arm across Ami's shoulders. I held her hand.

"Is there anything we can do?" Tariq Saleem asked.

"I am returning to the peninsula in a few days," he said. "My wife and I are helping to establish a child jockey rehabilitation center there. I will look for Umar. If I find him—or anyone I think might be him—I will take a photograph of him and have it faxed to you."

My mother looked over at Begum Naseem. She had no idea what Bashir was talking about. I must admit I was not quite sure either.

"I will give you my work fax number," Tariq Saleem said.

"Good," Mr. Bashir said. "Other than that, you can only wait. The sooner we find him, the better. It is against the law to use such young children as jockeys, but it still happens. Some trainers look for a small older boy whom they can use for show when the authorities come around."

At that point, Mr. Bashir looked over at me. "If you had a boy about Nadira's size," he said, "we could smuggle him in as one of those camel jockeys. He'd have a better chance of finding your son."

That was when I first got the idea, Umar. You may have already guessed what it is, but I won't write it down until I am certain. Because it could get me killed.

It could also save your life.

June 23

MY CHEEKS WERE BURNING all day. Not from a fever. It was like when I was first scarred. My whole body ached and trembled, as though my spirit didn't quite fit in it anymore. I felt that way again today.

Mayoun was upon us. Noor's relations poured into this house, like bright yellow flowers streaming out of a teakettle instead of masala chai. Mostly women, Noor's cousins. I could hear them teasing her for getting married in June. "Why do you always have to be different?"

When Duri came into the room, the women screamed for him to leave. Ami and I served the women lunch, tea, snacks, tea again, desserts. I have never seen people eat so much! They sang and sewed and put yellow paste—ubtan—on Noor. I didn't get to see all of it because I was busy cooking and waiting on people. Ami told me that Noor would not have to do much for the next few days, besides be paraded around in different outfits. Relatives would keep her company, feed her, entertain her.

"Was your wedding like this?" I asked our mother.

"It was a much simpler version of this," Ami said. "But it was very beautiful."

Somewhere in the middle of the day, Ami took me aside to say that Saliq's father had inquired about my marital status.

"I hope you told him I wasn't interested," I whispered.

"He didn't ask whether *you* were interested," Ami said.

"He must have asked about the scar," I said.

"He said Saliq did not want to know about the scar," Ami said, "but he said it was his responsibility as his father to find out."

I felt like I was going to throw up, Umar. I didn't want to think about any of this. I wanted you to come home. I did not want some old man trying to arrange a marriage between his son and me—a son who was probably being pushed into it.

"Ami, why are you talking about this now?" I asked our mother. "We have so much to do. And I want to figure out how to get Umar home, not how to get married."

"I told him it was an honor scar," she said. "I said your brother had been falsely accused, so the men of the village came after you. They did not take your virtue—because you struggled heroically—but they did scar you. He thanked me and went on his way."

I wanted to scream. I felt like I could not breathe—like I was in the village again.

"Did you tell him about my other scars?" I asked. "The one below my left breast. The one on my belly. The other one on my back."

"He does not need to know such things," Ami said.

"Did you tell him about the scar on my heart?"

"Shhh. I didn't know you would be so upset. I thought you would be excited! Come, we will speak of this later."

Later! Our mother did not understand. I had to go outside and take a deep breath. It was hot today. That

71

was why people usually did not get married in June.

I went back inside and served Noor and the women. Begum Naseem asked me if I was well. I nodded. I could not speak. I could not tell her I felt ill. Lost. I felt as though I was back in that village having pieces of my flesh carved away from my body.

As it turned dark, I had to go outside again. I could not stand to be inside with all the perfume and aromas and laughter. I was angrier than I had ever been in my life, Umar. Furious! I ran over to the tiny house and leaned against it. It was then that I saw Saliq up on a ladder hanging lights. I ran over to him.

"You had to send your father to find out what happened to me?" I shouted.

Saliq came down the ladder. "I'm sorry. What are you talking about?"

"Your father asked my mother about the scar, about what happened in the village!"

Saliq shook his head and looked at his hands. "I did not ask him to do that."

"So, you are *not* interested? You do not want to marry the scarred woman?"

"I—I told my father I liked you," he said. "I didn't know how to proceed, correctly."

"You *liked* me!"

"Yes, I wanted to hear the rest of the story."

"And so now you know, because your father asked. Are you still interested?"

"That wasn't the story I was interested in."

"You didn't answer my question."

"My father said you were attacked in the village because your brother had been falsely accused," he said. "There is no dishonor in that."

I laughed. I felt like I was watching myself. Just as I had that day in the village when it all happened.

"Yes, my mother tells people—when she must—that the men of the village came after me, this tiny twelve-year-old girl, but I was able to fight them off. I was brave and I was honorable and I saved my virtue and they were so angry they carved a moon on my face. But there's more, there is so much more. They carved me up here"—I pointed to the place beneath my breast—"and here." My belly. "Oh, and let's not forget my back."

I moved closer to Saliq, and he stepped away.

"I was twelve years old," I said. I was whispering now.
"Twelve years old. They were men. Dressed in white.
That kind of sparkling white you only see in the desert.
It's all lit up, that white, and they came after me. They
didn't even have to run. One of them caught my arm,
jerked me toward him. I struggled. They laughed, but I
could see they were angry. They stripped my little body
and then they took turns hurting my poor naked body.
One after another. They crumpled me into dust, and the
desert wind blew me away. When they were finished, they
took out their knives and left a mark on me. The father,
the two brothers, and the holy man. He left the one on my
cheek. That is the story. That is the rest of the story."

I had never told anyone that before. Ever. Even
myself. I looked Saliq straight in the eyes, as I had
never looked at any man besides Baba, and he looked
back. Only he was crying.

I turned away from him and vomited.

"I will get your mother," he said.

"No, no," I said, falling to my knees. "Some water."

I lay on the grass on my side until he returned.
Then I sat up and took the glass from him. He sat

beside me on the grass as I drank the water.

"What can I do?" he asked.

I handed the empty glass back to him and said, "Leave me alone."

Saliq hesitated, but then he got up and left. I waited several minutes before I returned to the house. I was careful not to let anyone see me while I looked around for scissors. I slipped them into my pocket and went to find our mother.

"I have to run an errand with Begum Naseem early tomorrow morning," I told her. "I'll sleep inside with Fatima so I won't wake you."

"All right, daughter," she said. "You look tired. Why don't you go rest now? It's been a long day."

I nodded, then hurried away and into the tiny house. I leaned over Ami's hand mirror, slipped off my scarf, grabbed a bunch of hair and began cutting. I didn't even cry, Umar. I was not sad—I was numb. I felt like a whirlwind. Yes, that was it. I felt as though the pieces of dust that had been me were coalescing into a whirlwind of intention. And my intention was to find my little brother and bring him home.

June 24

SOON MY HAIR WAS SHORT
and sticking out all over, just like a boy's. I carefully
braided the hair I had shorn and hid it in the tiny house.
I tried on Duri's old clothes until I found some that fit.
Then I took them off again and sewed pockets into the
inside of the tunic: one for your book and one for mine.
I wrapped tea leaves (along with some whole cloves and
cinnamon sticks) in paper and put them in a pouch. I
wrapped several dates and dropped them into the
pouch, too. I put it and a water skein around my neck.

Then I dressed in Duri's old clothes, and I dropped
a few coins I had saved into his pockets. I put my
clothes over his and fitted my scarf more tightly than

usual around my head and face to hide my short hair. I hid Duri's shoes and hat beneath my clothes as I hurried into the big house. My old room was empty, so I lay on my rug on the floor, closed my eyes and pretended to sleep.

Only I actually fell asleep. I awakened just after dawn. Fatima slept nearby. I heard no sounds of people, so I was certain I was the first awake. I hurriedly wrote our mother a note. It said, "Don't worry, Ami. I am safe. I will bring Umar home. With great affection, your daughter Nadira." I woke Fatima and pressed the note into her hand.

"Give this to my mother only if I do not return by nightfall," I said.

She sleepily agreed. I hurried out to the back, looked around, then crouched by the trash cans and took off my clothes—remember Duri's clothes were underneath. I put on his shoes and hat and threw my clothes in the trash. Then I hurried away.

I had memorized the address of the Children's Trust. I walked to a bus stop that was not far from Begum Naseem's house. Other people stood waiting too. I was so nervous, Umar. What if someone said something? What would happen to me? What would happen to you? I kept touching my scarless head. It felt odd. A man stared at me for a long time. I have never had that happen before. I almost ran away, but then I realized he was looking at my scar.

The bus came, and I asked the driver how to get to the Children's Trust. He just yelled, "Get on or get off." Someone tugged on my arm. I jumped down off the bus, and an old man told me to wait for the next bus. So I did. I could hear my heart pounding in my ears. I got on the bus with the old man. He even told me when to get off. As the bus pulled away, I stood looking around for a long while before I spotted the Children's Trust building. I ran across the street and hurried into the old building. It smelled damp, like it does everywhere during monsoon season.

I was surprised to find Mr. Bashir sitting at a paper-strewn desk in a small room where three of the walls were covered by bookshelves.

"Yes?" he asked, looking up at me.

"I—I am here about Umar, the kidnapped boy," I said.

"And who are you?"

I had not thought of what name to use! I almost said Ali Baba or Sindbad, but instead, I blurted out, "I'm Ali Akbar. I'm Umar's cousin."

"You can't be Rubel's son?" he said.

"No, another brother. But my father is dead. My auntie said you were looking for a boy about my size to go and help rescue the boys."

Bashir got up from his desk and came over to where I was standing.

"You're skinny," he said. "They might take you, even though you are too old. How old are you?"

"How old should I be?"

He laughed. "The law says the jockeys should all be over fourteen years of age, although I have never seen a jockey older than ten."

"I'm fifteen," I said.

"Why are you so small? And your voice so high?"

"There was trouble with my birth," I said.

He nodded. "These things happen. But I can't send a boy to do this." Bashir leaned against his desk. "It could be dangerous."

"I want to bring my cousin home," I said. "I'm really eighteen years old, but most people don't believe that."

"Still, it was a bad idea."

"Please, my aunt is a widow. She needs her son."

"How did you get that scar?" he asked.

"Someone insulted my cousin Nadira," I said. "I protected her. She was unharmed."

"So you know how to take care of yourself, then?" he asked. "The conditions are brutal at the camps. They beat the boys, starve them, make them work all the time. There is sexual abuse. They might not even take you to the same place where they took your cousin."

"I have to find my bro—my cousin. I have to bring him home. He's all my aunt has left."

"Well, I can't sanction this, but I will tell you we know where the men are who took your cousin."

"Does that mean Umar is still here?"

"No, these men just find the boys," Bashir said. "Someone else takes them away. You mustn't try to find out about your cousin from them. Just see if they're looking for anyone your age. I doubt anything will come of it."

Bashir handed me directions to where he thought the men might be. He also gave me his card with his phone numbers on it, as well as the address of the rehabilitation center on the peninsula.

As I started to leave, Bashir said, "I don't think this is a good idea. I should never have mentioned it. Please promise me you will go home to your aunt without looking for these men."

"I will be all right," I said. "Don't worry about me."

I left and walked freely through the streets—as I never had before—and no one noticed me! I got lost twice and had to stop and ask someone for directions, but I soon found the street and saw two men who fit the description of your kidnappers sitting outside a restaurant drinking tea.

I walked right up to them.

"Hello," I said. "I'm Ali Akbar, and I'd like to be a camel kid."

Umar, I thought they were going to strike me dead right there. One of them jumped up and grabbed my clothes and dragged me away. The other followed and kept shouting, "Keep it down! Not so much noise!"

They took me into an alleyway and pushed me to the ground.

"Who are you that you want to die so young?"

"I am sorry, sir," I said. "I am an orphan and need work. My Uncle Rubel sent me."

"Your uncle ought to be more careful," the shorter man said.

I stood slowly and brushed off my clothes.

"You're too old," the rough man said. "But you are light."

"Uncle Rubel said you needed older camel kids," I said. "Small ones. And strong. I'm very strong. And I've ridden a camel before."

The men looked at each other. I had ridden a camel once at a park Baba took us to. All I remembered was that the camel stank, but it seemed to like me. It kept trying to bite the other children waiting in line.

"I thought Rubel had changed his mind," the short man said. "He came looking for that other boy a few days ago."

"That was before he knew I wanted to go, too," I said.

Lying came more easily to me than I thought it would.

"He didn't tell us anything about another boy," the rough man said.

"The money doesn't go to him this time," I said. "It goes to my aunt, Bibi Mariam. I can give you her address."

"Yes, yes," the rough one said. "As it happens, we've got papers for an older kid."

"Will you send me to the same place as my cousin?" I asked. "It would be good to be around family."

"Of course," the short one said. "Be back here in an hour."

I felt I was guided on this day, Umar. I had found my way to your kidnappers, and they had accepted me! You would be in my arms soon, I was certain of it.

I waited not far from that spot, hidden, until the hour was done, and an old van pulled up to the two men. I got up and went to the van. The door slid open, and I saw it was crowded with young boys about your age, their dirty cheeks tearstained. One had his thumb in his mouth.

"Get in," the rough one told me.

The man at the wheel turned around, glanced at me, then looked away again. I got into the van. It stayed idling in the same spot for many minutes. The gasoline fumes wafted in through the open door, and several of the boys coughed. I could not see, but I could hear the rough man and the short man talking.

"Did your parents die too?" one little boy asked me.

"No talking!" the driver shouted.

I smiled at the boy but said nothing. I thought about grabbing one or two of the ten or more boys stuffed into that van and saving them, perhaps. Jumping out of the van and running. But I probably couldn't have gotten myself away, let alone them, so I stayed where I was, my heart thumping inside my chest.

Then I heard the rough one talking with someone out of my view. "Ah, your nephew is here," he said.

"My nephew?"

It was Rubel's voice.

I leaned over and pulled the door shut.

"Who said you could do that?" yelled the driver.

"It stinks," I said. I tried to wiggle back away from

the door, hoping against hope that Uncle Rubel would not see me.

"You said my nephew was gone," I heard Uncle Rubel say.

"Another one. Ali Akbar I think he called himself."

The driver beeped the horn.

"Say good-bye," the rough man said. The van door slid open. Uncle Rubel stood less than an arm's length from me. I put my head down.

"Hey you, show some respect," the rough one said. "Say good-bye to your uncle. Here." I looked up. The man dropped a small bag into my uncle's hand. "He wants it to go to his aunt Bibi Mariam. Makes no difference to me."

Rubel looked at me. His eyes opened wide—and then narrowed. If he told the men who I was, I was certain I would not see the next day. And why wouldn't he tell? Because he would have to return the money.

I looked him straight in the eyes.

"Have a safe trip, nephew," Rubel said, tossing the bag from one hand to another. Then he laughed.

A moment later the door slid shut again, and the van

load of boys—and me—raced away. I felt as though I could breathe again, despite the stink in that van. A couple of the boys threw up as the driver whipped the van around one corner after another. I yelled at him to open the window, and he told me to shut up. Finally he stopped the van. Someone opened the door, and two new men hurried us out of the vehicle and into an empty building.

I'm in that building now, in a room with twenty other people. I miss Ami and our tiny house. I miss the smell of jasmine. I wish I could see the rest of Noor's wedding, but I know that I will be with you soon, Umar, and that fact keeps me going.

PART TWO

Learn Wisely

July ?

I DON'T KNOW WHAT DATE IT is. I'm not certain of the passage of time. Oh, Umar. I have failed so completely. I still have not found you, and I believe I have put my own life and safety in jeopardy.

I am now writing in your little red book, "Learn Wisely." This is the first opportunity I have had to write in a long while. I could not risk it before. None of them can read, I am fairly certain, but I could be wrong. I shudder to think what would happen to me should someone discover my secret. I used the few coins I had to send the little green book to Ami. I gave it to a man at the airport, a man with a flower stand. I handed him the coins along with the book. I had penciled in Ami's address. I pleaded with him. I hope he did what I asked. I had to whisper. The men were busy with the younger children so I had only a moment.

That was many days ago. Maybe weeks? I have lost track of time. I think they drugged us at the building just before we left for the airport. They brought around tea, but it tasted strange, and I felt dizzy after. I knew I should run away then, but I couldn't manage to do anything except give my first book, the green book, to the man.

At the airport, two men and two women claimed all of us as their children. That was what our papers said, even though some of the children spoke a different language than their "parents."

In the days before we left for the airport, Talat— the little boy who asked me if my parents were dead— stayed close to me. He is smaller than you. I tried to figure out a way to get him away from the smugglers, but someone was at the door all the time, even when we slept.

They fed us runny white beans. I ate as little of it as

I could and instead sucked on the dates I had brought. I gave Talat one, too, along with Youssef. Youssef is a little older than the rest of the boys. I think he may have been picked for the same reason I was—to look good in case the authorities came around. He said he was twelve, but I think he is older.

Youssef said his father had sold him, but he had promised to visit him.

"Do you know where we're going, then?" I whispered.

"No," he said. "But my baba must." He looked frightened. "My baba must know where we're going, right?"

"I don't know," I said. I did not want to lie to these children. "I hope so. Every morning repeat your name to yourself. Every morning say the names of the members of your family. Say the name of the town where you lived. Before and after prayers say your name and the names of your relatives. Say it in your language. Don't forget your language."

They did not like us talking to one another, so we did not say much. More than once I wanted to run away, Umar. But I kept thinking of you in a place like this without a big sister (or big brother) to look after you.

Then they gave us the tea, and I felt dizzy and sleepy. They drove us to the airport. I had never been to the airport. I wanted to be excited by it, but I felt half asleep. All the children shuffled around the same way. None of them cried. The so-called parents held the hands of some of the children. I tried to keep Talat close to me. When we went by the flower stand, I saw a man with kind eyes, so I pressed the green book into his hands and quietly (and quickly) pleaded with him. I could not wait to see what he said or did. One of the men grabbed me by the ear and pushed me back into the group of children.

We got on the plane. Soon after I heard a roar. My stomach felt light. When I looked out the window, I saw we were over land. I wanted to remember every detail so that I could tell you, and we could compare when we were together again. But I could not keep my eyes open. Talat had already fallen asleep with his little self leaning against me. I did not know where Youssef was. They only let Talat stay with me because he would cry otherwise. I did not know how long we flew or what we flew over. I thought of the magic carpet from the

Arabian Nights and decided it would be more fun than this sleepy plane ride. I fell right to sleep.

We landed in the desert, this I know. In Bedouin land, I was certain. The blond sand cascaded this way and that, like a giant scarf wrapped around a woman's head and shoulders. I kept tripping over my feet as I walked away from the plane toward a white van. I picked up Talat because he was still sleeping, like I used to pick you up when you were younger. I was afraid I would drop him, but we were soon in the van. Our drugged weariness sharpened into nausea, and nearly all the boys began vomiting. I won't describe any more of that trip. I don't really want to think of it. Sometime later, the van stopped at the camel-training camp.

The driver of the van pushed us out of the vehicle and into the desert. Everywhere I turned I saw desert, camels, and young boys. A roaring man came out from one of the tin shacks scattered about the camp. Yes, he roared, Umar. Like a wild animal. We shrank back from him. Talat whimpered and ran behind me.

"I am Zaid, and you will do whatever I tell you or I will beat you. The first time. The second time you disobey me, I will take you out in the desert and leave you for vultures that will pick your bones dry while you are still alive."

He had a thick accent, so I wasn't certain if everyone understood his words, but they knew his intent. In the near distance, other boys watched us. They were all small. Many stood with arms crossed, and their faces looked hard, like men. I squinted, looking for you, but you were not among these first faces.

Our group was separated into three groups of five. One of the older boys showed the five of us to a shack where we would sleep at night. It was hot, dark, and smelly inside. A dirty blanket and piece of carpet covered the floor of sand here and there.

The older boy took us to a ditch behind the shacks: our latrine. I had never seen anything like it, Umar, and hope to never see or smell anything like it again. He warned us not to go out into the desert because of the deadly snakes and even deadlier insects.

"And hungry bandits wait out in the desert for little children to snack on," he said.

The boy led us to the camel barn where we would

be working. It was big and airy, long and rectangular.

"Ten camels here," the boy said, although no camels were in the barn. "You take care of them. Make certain the water and food troughs are clean. Always water. Brush them. No bugs. Feed them special food. Take them out. Bring them back."

He pointed to the shovels. "Go to work now." He sounded like a native speaker to our tongue, yet his words came in spurts, as though he had forgotten how to speak.

"You." He tugged on my sleeve. "I show you. You show them." We walked to the end of the barn and into a room that was cooler than the rest of the barn, which meant they somehow had electricity out here. Isn't that strange? We didn't have electricity in our place next to Rubel, but these people had electricity here for their camels. The boy showed me huge bins of barley, oats, dates, and greens, plus large glass bottles of pills. The boy put barley, oats, dates, and several pills into a big blue bucket. Out of one of the smaller bins he pulled a bulb of garlic and dropped it into the strange meal. He put the bucket under a faucet and squirted a creamy liquid into it. He stirred the concoction with a stick and then carried it to one of the camel troughs, and tipped it in. Next he dropped a pile of greens next to the barley mash.

"Two times a day for the camels. If you eat, you die. Poison. Only for camels. Now you."

We went back to the bins, and I tried to emulate what the boy had just done. I got it exactly right. I have Ami to thank for that—all those times I watched her cook. The boy showed us the saddles and halters and told us we had to keep them clean, organized, and ready to use.

When the boy finished, Zaid came in and screamed at us in a language I did not understand. This sent us running out in the direction he pointed, toward the training track. Several camels ran around a track that was just a place in the sand marked off by a kind of fence. The camels rocked back and forth when they ran, Umar, which I'm sure you noticed if you are somewhere like this—although I pray you are somewhere safer! On the back of each of these camels was a young boy clinging to the strap around the animal's hump.

Compared to the huge animals, the boys looked so tiny! A white truck drove alongside the fence while a man hung out the window screaming at the boys.

I did not have long to watch. Zaid kicked and pushed me until I understood what he wanted. I took the rope of one camel and started back to the barn. Zaid screamed at me until I held the ropes of three of these giants. I didn't have time to notice anything about the camels. I was too busy trying to understand Zaid and not get kicked by him. I knew he could speak our language because he had earlier, but now he refused. In the chaos that ensued, I figured out the food needed to be ready for the camels by the time they returned to the barn. They ate while we brushed them down. Then we had to make certain the saddles were dry as well as dust and bug free. This may not sound like much, but these animals were so big, and we were small! None of us knew what we were doing. We were quite disorganized. After a while, other boys came and watched, then laughed at us. It was the hottest time of the day, and I felt sick to my stomach from lack of food and water.

The camels had a peculiar smell. I can't describe it

truly. Like sweat, sour milk, and a damp room, I suppose. One vomited in Talat's direction, and he screamed. Then he cleaned it up. He's a good boy.

Finally we finished our work, and we returned to eat with the other new boys. Most of them were too tired to cry. We sat huddled beneath what little shade the shacks provided.

After we ate, we went back to the barn and kept working. By night, I was ready to sleep. I noticed the boys seemed more tired than I was—even Youssef who was bigger than the younger boys. I decided it was because they were boys and had been used to being spoiled even though their parents were poor. I felt superior for my endurance until I remembered that you, my dear brother, are also a poor pampered boy! Then I took a few of the dates from my pouch and passed them around to the four boys with me. Malik and Suleiman are brothers from a village near the mountains in our country. They had been playing near their home when two passing tradesmen offered them fruit. When the brothers awakened, they were far from home in some strange city on their way here.

The smugglers told them their parents were dead.

"My parents are dead too," Talat said when the brothers told us their story.

"Did the smugglers tell you that?" I asked.

He nodded.

"None of your parents are dead," I said. "You were stolen." I wanted to tell the boys I would figure out a way to get them home, but I knew I could not promise such a thing.

"I have an idea about tomorrow," I said. "We kept bumping into each other when we were trying to do things today. Malik and Talat are too small to carry those heavy buckets, so I think they should take the hay and greens to the camels while we're getting the mash. Here's how we can do it. There are five buckets, right? It'll be like preparing a meal. We'll line up the buckets and one of us will put in the grains, dates, and garlic. Those are all in bins. The other person will drop in the pills. The third person will squirt in the milk, or whatever that is. Then we'll each take a bucket to a camel. The first one back will grab the fourth bucket, the second one the fifth bucket. The third person will start preparing the next five buckets with the three buckets now there empty. Does that make sense?"

The boys stared at me.

"I'll show you tomorrow," I said. "Then the three stronger boys—me, Suleiman, and Youssef—will clean up the dung while Talat and Malik brush the camels. You could reach using the stools?" They nodded.

As it grew darker, the men I had seen throughout the day disappeared. Perhaps they stayed in apartments in the barns or they had better shacks somewhere. I didn't know. We ate our meager meals of bread and runny beans—brought to us by a man in a truck with a pot, a ladle, and a common plate. As we finished, I heard something that sent shivers through my body.

It was the sound of feet running through sand. I remembered that sound—or one like it—from when we lived in the village. When the men came after me. Only I had been the one running. Now my heart raced.

"Quickly," I said to the boys. "Inside!"

I ran into the shack and felt around in the dark for something to put up across the entrance—or at least for something sharp we could use for protection. I found only sand and blanket. And quiet. The four boys became so quiet. Outside I heard a squeal, like an animal—only I knew it was a boy.

"In the corner," I whispered. "Maybe they'll think we're gone."

"If they come after us," Youssef said, "try to gouge out their eyes or crush their testicles."

"Yes, right," I said.

We crouched down as a group and pressed ourselves up against the back wall. Talat started to cry.

"You must be quiet, little Talat," I said, putting my arm across his shoulder. "We will do our best to protect you, but for now you must be quiet."

Outside someone screamed. I thought I heard fists on flesh. A peculiar quiet thudding. I closed my eyes and tried not to remember the sounds from the village. How quiet everything had been, except for me screaming and then whimpering.

Whatever was happening out in that night now, it could not happen to me. I couldn't go through it again. This time I would not survive, once they knew my secret.

"Please let Umar be safe," I prayed. "Please let Umar be safe."

The night grew quiet again. The five of us stayed together for a long while in that corner. Then we moved away, each to a blanket, and fell asleep.

Second Day at the Camel Camp

I AWAKENED PREDAWN TO SAND in my face and screams in my ear. I sat up gasping. One of the older boys from yesterday yelled and kicked at us. He, too, now spoke another language.

We ran to the barn. Once there, the older boy disappeared. I reminded the two smaller boys that they were going to start by feeding the greens to the camels. The rest of us began "cooking" breakfast. Suleiman and Youssef quickly caught on to my idea, and we fed the camels in no time. The two smaller boys cleaned and brushed the camels, while the rest of us shoveled away the dung.

Three older boys came and put saddles on five of the camels and led them away.

We were allowed to go back to our shack, where someone came by with bread and beans again. We sat on the sand with the other new boys. Three of them had bruises on their faces.

"What happened?" I asked quietly.

"What do you think happened?" one of them said. "The other boys showed us who is boss of this camp. Your turn will come."

Then the five of them moved away from us and ate by their shack.

We returned to the barn and cleaned it, then we brushed the camels.

During the hottest part of the day when most of the boys napped, I went around the camp looking for you, Umar.

I ran from shack to shack and looked inside to see if you were there. Many boys were sleeping, but some were not, and I saw things I never want to see again. Some bigger boys beat smaller boys. They were so quiet, these beatings. Just the sound of flesh against flesh. And some of the older boys attacked the smaller boys the way those men in the village attacked me. The little boys could not escape, just as I could not. I wanted to save them, Umar. I did. But I could not risk getting caught. So I ran back to our shack, went inside, and cried quietly. I hoped the big boys would not leave scars on the bodies of the little boys like the men in the village had left on me. I hoped their bodies would not be covered with little broken moons for the rest of their lives as a constant reminder of what had happened to them. That is not a happy way to live.

I realized then how foolish I was to come here. It was going to happen to me again—just as it had at the village—only this time I would not live, I was certain of it. And what of these boys who were hurting other boys? They had all once been sweet children. The evil things they did now were not their fault. They had come here when they were so young, and now they knew no other way, no other life.

How was I going to keep it from happening to me and the four boys who were with me?

Once again, I was exhausted when night came, and the boys were worse off than I was. I gave them the last of the dates. Then the air grew still. We heard the sound of feet running over sand, saw shadows moving across the desert, like ghosts coming to claim their victims. We ran into the shack. I had "borrowed" three of the sticks we used to stir the mash. (If someone discovered the temporary theft, we would be severely beaten, so I had to remember to put them back.) I handed one to each of the older boys and kept one for myself.

Again we heard the sound of thuds, crying, a scream. It sounded closer than it had the night before. When it was quiet again, Talat wept.

"I want my ami," he said.

"I know, I know," I said. I could feel the other boys next to me shivering.

"They're going after the new boys," Youssef said. "Tomorrow night it'll be us."

"I know," I said.

Talat leaned up against me, his tiny body trembling.

"Let's think of something else," I said. "We're safe now." For a while. "How about a story? Maybe that'll help us relax so we can think of what we can do tomorrow night. Have you heard the story of Abu Hasan?"

It was the first story that came to mind, Umar, because I told it to you a few weeks after Baba died. He loved telling that story.

"There was a man, Abu Hasan, who left the wandering life to become a merchant," I said. "He was very good. He only sold the softest silks, the most magnificent carpets, the headiest perfume. He became a very rich man and decided it was time to marry. An old woman who does those things found him a wife who was very beautiful. He opened up his house and invited friends to a magnificent feast. They had rice of many different colors and sherbets of many different flavors. They ate roasted lamb and even—" I leaned down close to Talat's ear and said "—roasted camel! The night wore on and finally it was time for Abu Hasan to go to the bridal chamber where his wife awaited him. The men all shouted for him to go. So he got up from his chair and something terrible happened!"

"What?" Suleiman asked. "Did his friends attack him?"

"Did his bride run away?" Youssef asked.

"He found out his parents had died?" Talat asked.

"No, what happened was far worse," I said. "Abu Hasan rose up from his chair and he . . . let go a fart! Oh, the embarrassment! Abu Hasan's guests all pretended they had heard nothing. Abu Hasan hurried away, as though he was going to his bride after all, but instead he left the house, got on his horse, and rode away, crying all the while, until he reached the water where he got on a ship and sailed away to a foreign land. In this strange land, Abu Hasan did well again, making friends with many a great man. But after ten years, he longed for home. He could not bear another day away from his beloved homeland. Without a word to anyone, he left and headed for his native land. He went through many hardships. He had to travel over mountains, he lost his money, he nearly starved, he nearly died of thirst. He went through one terrible day to the next until one day he was looking down on the hills of home! He was so happy.

"However, Abu Hasan was still concerned about coming home. Would people remember? How could they? It had been ten years. Nevertheless, he stayed disguised for seven days and seven nights, while he walked around town listening and watching."

"One day, he happened to be sitting outside a home when he heard a young girl inside inquire, 'Mother, could you tell me the day I was born so that I may have my fortune told?' Her mother said, 'That is easy, child. You were born on the night when Abu Hasan farted at his wedding feast.' Upon hearing those words, Abu Hasan jumped up and ran away again, saying, 'My fart has become a date that will be remembered until the end of time.' He returned to the land of his exile and there remained until the end of his life."

Talat had stopped shaking. He lay with his head in my lap, asleep. Youssef picked him up and put him on his blanket in the sand, and then we all lay down.

As I closed my eyes, I heard Suleiman whispering, "'It will be a date remembered until the end of time.'" He and his brother giggled softly. I smiled and hoped you were safe and well, Umar.

Third Day

AT BREAKFAST, I SAW THE BRUISES on some of the boys from the second new group. I was certain it would be our turn tonight. I had to find some way to protect us.

In the heat of the day, I looked around for something to make a door for our shack. I ran from barn to barn, but I could not find anything useful—and several boys chased me away from each barn. When it was nearly time to go back to our barn and camels, I went into the desert to relieve myself. (I need to be careful and make certain no one follows me when I do this. I have seen the bigger boys follow the smaller boys.) When I was finished, I saw a spot of red on one of the hills of sand, so I ran to it, slip-sliding all the way up, until I grabbed the red and tugged on it. The sand fell away easily. I pulled and pulled until I was looking at a strange kind of net made of red flexible plastic. I balled it up as best I could and ran back to our shack.

"What is it?" Youssef asked as he and the three boys followed me inside the shack. I unrolled the netting and showed it to them.

"Our door," I said.

Youssef nodded, understanding immediately. We held it up to the entrance; it would cover it and then some. Hurrying, we hooked the netting onto the tacks and nails that held the shack together near the entrance. We would finish closing it up after dark.

None of the new boys ate with us anymore. Each group had separated and now inhabited their own sphere of suffering. That night, the five of us took our food into the shack and put up the netting. After we had tied it and looped it onto the nails, we dug out the sand for about a foot in front of the netting, buried the bottom part of it in the hole, then covered it with sand again. When we were finished, Youssef ran into it. It held.

Then we sat and waited. Talat held my hand, but he did not cry.

Darkness.

The thumping across the sand.

Shadows at our door.

A groan as someone ran into the netting.

"What is this?" a boy shouted, frustrated.

Another boy ran into it.

"Some magic thing they have put up!" one of the boys cried.

Another boy tried to get in. The shack trembled. Would they just tip it over?

I got to my feet and whispered to Talat and the others, "Be ready to run."

Then one shadow stood at the netting without trying to get in.

"This is no magic," the shadow boy said. "We will get you tomorrow."

I stepped closer to the door. "If you touch any of us—"

"What? What will you do?" the shadow boy asked. "I am already dead."

I could not see his eyes clearly, but I knew he spoke the truth.

"May the mercy of Allah be upon you," I said.

"Don't curse me, boy. It will do you no good. We rule this place."

"I see no rulers here," I said.

"Tomorrow I will show you, personally."

Then he was gone, along with the other shadows. The camp was silent again.

"What are we going to do?" Talat asked.

"I'm not sure," I said.

"They'll just come get the door when we're not here tomorrow," Youssef said.

"Yes, so we'll take it down in the morning and hide it in the barn," I said. "We'll put it up again tomorrow night, but by the time they get in we will be gone."

"What do you mean?" Suleiman asked.

"We'll make a tunnel here and go out the back and hide in the barn," I said.

"But what will we do the next night?" Youssef asked.

"I'm not sure," I said. "We'll figure that out later."

We spent the next couple of hours digging until we made a hole just big enough for us to crawl out of the shack. In the morning, we quickly took down the door and covered the hole, inside and out, with blankets. I hid the netting behind the bins in the barn.

By the end of the day, we were almost too exhausted to shuffle back to the shack, but we did. We ate quickly, then went inside our shack. Darkness was falling fast, and we could hear boys at the other end of the camp calling out, like women at a wedding. My heart beat so hard in my chest I could barely hear anything else. As soon as we got the netting up, the five of us quietly slid out of the shack through the hole we had made the previous night. Youssef and I quickly kicked the dirt back in the hole. Then I took Talat's hand, and we quietly ran toward the barn. We could still hear the boys shouting, so we knew they were not after us yet.

Once at the barn, we tiptoed inside. We were not allowed in the barn at night, but I didn't see or hear anyone else inside the darkened building who would challenge us. We walked along the side, away from the camels and toward the grain bins. The camels grunted, chewed, breathed. The boys and I held hands and moved along the walls as fast as we could without running into something.

Only I tripped over a bucket.

We stopped and listened as the noise died away.

The camels didn't seem to care.

We hurried into the room where the bins were. I closed the door behind us.

"There's no lock," Youssef whispered.

"We'll use our bodies," I said.

The five of us sank to the floor and leaned against the door.

I listened but heard nothing besides the breathing of the children next to me.

One by one, the boys fell asleep. I slept off and on. Waiting. Waiting.

Our trick must have fooled them. Before dawn, I awakened the boys. I gave them each two dates from the camel bins.

"They're poison!" Talat said.

"No, I had one the first day," Youssef said. "They just don't want us to eat them."

We fed the camels. Then the younger boys groomed them while Youssef and I shoveled dung. Zaid and one of the older boys came running into the barn. Zaid's face was purple, Umar. Purple! He was so angry.

"What happened to your hut?" he demanded.

"I don't know what you mean, sir," I said. "We left early to get to work."

"It has collapsed," Zaid said. "Did you do that?"

"No," I said. "It must have fallen after we left."

"Well, you'll have to put it back up, or you can sleep out on the sand like so many of the boys do."

"But, sir, we won't have time to put it up before—"

"Before what?"

"Before night."

"Not my problem!" Zaid turned and left the barn. The older boy watched us for a moment before he followed Zaid. I wondered if he was one of the shadow boys.

The five of us looked at one another.

What were we going to do now?

"We could try to convince the other children to go

after the shadow boys," Youssef said, "and get them before they get us."

"That would all take time," I said, "and we don't have any time. Besides I don't believe brute force would work."

Instead, I had to use what I knew. "Learn wisely."

I went over to the pill bottles. One was almost empty, so I dumped the last pills into a new bottle.

"Are you going to break it and make weapons?" Youssef asked.

"No," I said, "I'm going to make tea."

I got out my pouch and dropped part of the tea leaves into the now-empty glass bottle. I put several cloves and a piece of cinnamon into it. Then I mashed a date and added it. I ran to the faucet by the trough, turned it on, and filled the bottle with water. Then I screwed on the cap. When it was time for breakfast, I hid the bottle as best I could under my clothes. With the boys surrounding me, we ran toward the shack, which now lay almost flat on the ground. We spent a few minutes trying to get the shack up again. It worked—we got it up—but it would not withstand another attack until we did more work on it. I put the tea bottle in the full sun in a spot where I thought it would remain unobserved.

We ate breakfast, then ran to the camel barn to complete our day.

Since we had had little sleep and even less food, we could barely walk to the shack at the end of the day. I grabbed the tea bottle and brought it into the shack. I took a sip. It was not the best tea in the world but given the shadow boys had probably not had tea in years, it would do fine. We put the netting up across the entrance again. I prayed that what I was doing would work. I didn't know what else to do. We were too exhausted to keep running every night—and they would figure out where we had been hiding soon enough.

I stood at the door, waiting. Youssef stayed next to me.

The sun fell. I heard it sizzling on the ocean of sand. Pink blanketed the world. For an instant. Then it was night.

Silence.

Then the thumping.

The shadow boys ran to our door but stopped when they saw me waiting.

"I will speak to the one," I said.

The shadow boys parted and the one I had talked to the night before came up to the netting.

"I would like to strike a bargain," I said.

"You have nothing to offer," he said.

"I might," I said. "My mother was known for her masala chai. It is said to have magical properties. How long has it been since you had tea?"

"You have tea?"

"I do."

"I could come and take it from you," he said.

"It will be emptied into the sand if you try to obtain it by force," I said. "But I will offer it to you and more."

"What else?"

"I ask that you sit and drink the tea and listen to a story," I said. "If the story interests you and you wish to hear the end, then you will leave us in peace."

I could feel the shadow boy staring at me.

"It is a deal," he said.

"Then you must move away," I said. "All of you, and sit on the sand while I prepare the tea."

The shadow boy shouted to his boys to sit in the sand. Then he slowly backed away. Youssef undid the netting. My heart was in my throat again, Umar. I did not trust the shadow boy, but I had to try this. We had told Talat and Malik to stay in the shack, in the corner, in case something went wrong—I hoped they would forget about the little boys if they decided to hurt me, especially after they discovered my secret.

Suleiman stepped forward and put the thickest blanket on the sand.

"Your seat of honor," I said to the shadow boy.

He kept standing. Youssef dropped another blanket at the entrance to the shack, and I sat on it. Youssef sat behind me. Then the shadow boy sat across from me. My heart sounded like a drum. Youssef had found something resembling a cup earlier and when I nodded to him, he poured the sun tea into the cup and handed it to me. I held the cup out to the shadow boy.

"First you," he said.

I took a sip. He watched me. I handed him the cup. He grabbed it and took a swallow. Then he gulped.

"More," he said.

We filled the cup again. This time he sipped the tea.

"And so?" he said.

"And so," I said, "a young woman married a man who was a great traveler. On one journey, he was gone a long while, and the woman grew lonely. She met and fell in love with a young man, and he returned her love. As it happens, this young man got in a fight with another man and was thrown in prison. When the woman discovered what had happened to her lover, she put on her finest clothes and went to the chief of police and said, 'My brother so and so has been falsely accused and is now in prison. Please help me get him released!' Now, ordinarily the Chief was not very helpful in these sorts of cases, but as soon as he saw this woman he was smitten, and he had to have her. 'I can sign this paper,' he said, 'and that will start the process, but first may we step into my chamber?' The woman knew what the Chief wanted from her, but she said, 'Oh, my lord, this is so public. Will you not stop by my house at such and such at this time?' 'I will sign the paper then,' he agreed.

"Next the woman went to the Kazi—the man in charge of the whole city—and said, 'My brother has been falsely accused, and I beg you to help with his release by signing this paper, which the Chief has promised to sign, too.' Now, the Kazi was not usually a man to help people with any of their problems, but as soon as he saw our lady, he fell in love and wanted her for himself. 'I will, lady,' he said, 'if you would be so kind as to step into my chamber.' 'Oh, my lord,' she said. 'It is so public. Why not come to my home at such and such at this time?' And she named a time only a few minutes after the hour she had told the Chief to come."

I looked at the shadow boy and all the shadow boys around him. They were quiet, listening. The shadow boy sipped his tea and nodded.

"Next our lady went to the King and said, 'Oh, my lord, my brother has been falsely accused and is now in prison. Will you sign his release as the Kazi and Chief have promised so that I may show it to the treasurer and ensure my brother's release?' The King did not often help people with their problems, but when he saw our lady, he immediately fell in love and had to have her. 'I will do as you ask,' the King said, 'but first will you step into my chamber?' 'Ah, my lord,' she said. 'It is so public. Will you not come to my home at such and such at this time?' And she named a time not far from the Kazi's time of arrival. The King was not so easily put off as the others had been, but eventually he let the woman leave.

"She immediately went to the carpenter and asked if he could make four cabinets, one on top of the other, with locks on them. The carpenter said, 'I can surely fashion you the best cabinets in all the land.' 'How much will it cost?' she asked. The carpenter was not someone who helped out people in trouble, but he, like all the others, had fallen in love with the beautiful woman. 'It will cost you nothing if you step into my back room with me,' he said. 'Gladly,' she said, 'but it is so public. Bring the cabinets to my house and leave them where I wish. Then return later that evening and I will feed you.' He agreed. The woman went home. Later the carpenter came and brought the cabinets and left them. Soon after, someone knocked on the door. She opened it and found the Chief there and—."

I stopped and breathed deeply. "That is the end of the tale until tomorrow."

The desert throbbed with silence.

The shadow boy tipped the dregs of his tea into his mouth and handed the cup back to me. He stood. My breath caught in my throat. He clapped his hands twice, and the other boys stood and ran away like ghosts in the sand.

"Tomorrow," he said.

Then he, too, was gone.

Youssef patted my shoulder. "You are a strange boy, Akbar, but you have saved us this night."

"We'll see," I said. And we stitched up the net door again.

I did not sleep well. Every time I heard a noise, I sat upright, but no one accosted us. We made it through another night.

Day Four (???)

IN THE MORNING, I SIPPED A bit of the tea myself. Then the five of us went to the barn and did our work. At breakfast the other two groups of new boys came over to us.

"Did you hurt them?" one of the boys asked.

"Yes, did you kill them all?" another pleaded.

"No," Youssef said, "we gave them tea and told them stories."

The boys stared at us.

"You should have killed them."

"Tonight I will tell another story," I said. "You may all come. We'll light a barrel. It will be good."

The day passed quickly. We ate our dinner, and the

other boys came around our shack. Someone dragged a barrel over and lit it. The smell of oil permeated the air, and I was sorry I had suggested it, yet the light was strangely soothing. As it grew darker, the faces of the boys became golden from the flames.

Then the shadow boys came. The one I had made the bargain with sat on the blanket near me. I handed him a cup of tea. Then I said, "And so, the young woman had invited four men over in an effort to get her lover out of jail. The first man arrived. He was the Chief of Police. She invited him in, praised him, and then sat on the couch with him. He began kissing her. She said, 'Oh, my lord, will you sign this first, so that we may not forget? Then take off your clothes while I fetch you something to eat.'"

Some of the boys giggled here. I started to breathe a little easier.

"The Chief quickly signed the release, and then hurriedly threw off his clothes. No sooner had the Chief taken off all his clothes when there was a knock on the door. 'Who is that?' the Chief asked. 'Oh! It is my husband,' the woman said. 'Quick. Hide in this top cabinet.'

And the woman pushed him toward the cabinet before he could grab his clothes. He climbed in, and she locked him inside.

"She went to the door and let in the Kazi. She praised him and then sat on the couch with him. He began kissing her, until she said, 'Oh, my lord, will you sign this release so that we may not forget? Then take off your clothes so that we may enjoy ourselves. I will fetch you something to eat.' He signed the form and had his clothes all off when someone knocked on the door. The woman picked up the Kazi's clothes as he said, 'Who is that?' 'It is my husband, lord. Hide in this second cabinet until I can get rid of him.' The naked man did as he was told, and the woman locked the second cabinet door.

"She opened the door and invited in the King. She praised him and kissed his feet. They sat on the couch together and he began kissing her. 'Oh, my King, will you sign the release so that we may not forget as we partake in all earthly pleasures? And then take off your clothes so we may enjoy ourselves. I will fetch you some food and drink.' The King quickly signed and then pulled off his clothes, tossing them here and there.

When he was naked, someone knocked on the door. 'Who is that?' the King asked. 'Oh, my lord, it is my husband.' 'Tell him to go away or I will kill him.' 'No, no, let me handle it my way, please,' she said. 'Just wait in this bottom cabinet while I get rid of him.' The King reluctantly agreed. As soon as he was inside, she locked the cabinet and went to the door.

"She let the carpenter in. 'I am afraid your work was not very good,' the woman said. 'This cabinet is not as big as I wanted. I was not able to get into it, so how will my servants be able to properly store my dishes inside?' 'Impossible!' he said. 'It is big enough for three men. I will demonstrate.' And so he crawled into the third cabinet, and the woman locked him in.

"Then the woman packed all her things and went to the prison where she showed the signed document to the prison treasurer. He immediately released her lover. They hurried out to the woman's wagons where she told her lover all that she had done to earn his release. 'What now then, pray?' he asked. 'We will travel far from here!' the woman said. And they left and were never seen in this city again.

"Meanwhile, three days went by without the men eating or drinking. They all tried to hold their water, but finally, the Chief could bear it no longer! He urinated on the Kazi and the Kazi urinated on the carpenter and the carpenter urinated on the King. 'Who makes water on me?' cried the Kazi. 'Kazi?' the Chief said. 'Chief! Oh, that woman has tricked the most important officials in the city. I am thankful the King is not here.' The King said, 'Hold off on the praises. I am here, too.' Then they all began making loud noises until the neighbors drew near. After a time the neighbors came into the house and stood by the cabinets. 'I think she has trapped a jinni in there,' one of the neighbors said. 'Let us get fuel and burn it down!' 'Wait!' cried the Kazi. 'We are mortal men. Let us out!' And the four men gave their names and someone recognized their voices and let them out of the cabinets. The four men stood naked before the neighbors. They looked at one another and began laughing. What a trick the lady had played on everyone!"

I looked over at the shadow boy. He held out the cup. I handed it back to Youssef, who refilled it. The glass bottle would soon be empty. The shadow boy sipped the tea and nodded to me. I knew we were not safe yet. So I began the tale of Sindbad. I started with his first voyage. Yes, Umar, I changed it some, just as I had with the woman—remember, she had five suitors. I described the ship of Sindbad's first voyage. How it was filled with the most beautiful and expensive cargo, how they stopped at an island to rest, and then suddenly someone told them to run for their lives: It was no island but a giant fish! The island fish sank and drowned most everyone on it, but Sindbad got away and ended up in another land, even more bewitching. But the story of that land was saved for the next night.

The boys all left, except for the shadow boy.

"Do we have a bargain, then?" I asked him.

"We do," he said.

"Even after the tea runs out?"

"Yes," he said, as though he was relieved, as though he had been looking for a reason—any reason—to stop what he had been doing. "At night they cannot control us."

"Then let's do something else with the nights," I

said. "Why be like them at night? Maybe we can protect ourselves better if we work together."

"Perhaps," he said. "Does Sindbad ever get home again?"

"We will see," I said.

And that was how we saved ourselves, Umar. At least for then. Every night the boys gathered, and I told part of a story. I stretched the Sindbad story for many nights—I even added a few voyages he never made. It did not make life perfect, but at least we were able to sleep at night without too much worry. The days were still filled with little food and too many kicks and slaps.

Many Days and Nights

THE DAYS WENT THE SAME FOR
a long time, Umar. The camels in our barn were very
well-behaved. We never hit them, and I always talked to
them. I encouraged the boys to talk to them, too. Zaid figured out I had an affinity with the camels, so he put
camels they had problems with in our barn. I did not
mind. Camels are like any other living creature: they need
food, water, rest, and affection. I did the best I could.

It grew hotter. It soon became clear that you were
not here and you were not coming here. Why endure
this misery if I was not helping you? I watched everything that went on in the camp so that I could discover
safe passage to another camp.

The camels in our barn were all going to race this year. In other barns, boys trained younger camels to get used to the saddle and a jockey. A man in white, a Bedu, was often there to tell Zaid what to do. He was either the owner or the trainer.

After a while, Zaid started to put Talat and Malik on the camels. On his first time up, Talat looked over at me, his eyes filling with tears, and I stared back at him, trying to encourage him without saying a word. Oh, Umar, it about broke my heart to see these children treated so inhumanely day after day. My goal was to save you. After that, I needed to save them. Talat and Malik were tied to the saddle at first. They also held on to the strap around the hump. Zaid walked the camels for a while, and then he had them go faster, so the boys could get used to the camels' gait—or so the camel could get used to the boy.

At the end of that first day of riding, Talat and Malik returned to the shack crying and holding on to their testicles. They were so sore, and I had nothing to help them. Nothing cold. No ointment. Youssef had gotten good at finding things for us—with the help of

Shadow Boy, I suspected—so I asked him to try and find some extra cloth (or clothes), and a needle and thread. I took turns rocking the two little boys on my lap until it was time for a story. Then they lay in the shack, curled up next to each other while I continued the tale of "Ali Baba and the Forty Thieves."

To my surprise, Youssef was able to procure the needed items within a day, in exchange for a few dates.

"Why don't they just steal dates from their own barns?" I asked.

"Because they believe they're poisoned," Youssef said. "They also believe that you have the gift of removing poison, so they know your dates are safe. A boy was caught with his hand in the dates once, and Zaid made him eat one and the boy fell ill within minutes. They think you're a sorcerer. Or jinni. The boy with the enchanted scar."

I spent that night—after the story—making pouches for the boys that would cover their testicles. I stuffed sand inside these pouches and then sewed them up again. The next day the three boys—Suleiman was riding now too—wore the pouches and came back feeling much less bruised. I made two more, one for me and one for Youssef.

Within a few days, word had gotten around camp about the pouches. All the riders wanted one, even though most of them were barely old enough to say out loud what they wanted. We had plenty of sand: that would not be a problem. But Shadow Boy and Youssef had to work hard to find enough thread, needles, and cloth. I couldn't do it alone, of course, so I taught many of the boys how to sew. The younger boys could not get their fingers to thread the needle and make the loops through the cloth, but the older boys could do it and did. At night we set up several barrels of light during stories. While I told tales, many of the boys sewed pouches. It was quite a sight, Umar, me talking while these boys sewed. In those moments, as Shadow Boy and Youssef passed around watered-down tea and the boys sewed and listened, we could pretend all was normal—or at least a kind of normal we had decided to create for ourselves.

Yet I was not getting any closer to you, Umar. Often I sat out under a night sky filled with stars wondering where you were. For several nights in a row, I saw many falling stars. I called the boys out of their shelters to watch with me. I told them Baba's story of the Fallen Star Children.

"So many stars are falling tonight," Talat said. "Do you think they will all find their families again?"

"I hope so," I said.

"They look like they're falling to the desert," Suleiman said. "Do you think Zaid will make them ride camels?"

"Maybe we should go find them first," Talat said. "I bet they'd be easy to spot in the desert at night. If they're still shiny and bright." Suleiman and Talat stood alongside several other boys, ready to begin the rescue.

"That's nice of you to want to save any lost children," I said, "but you need to keep yourselves safe."

"It's just a story!" Youssef said. "There are no lost children in the desert!"

"No?" Shadow Boy said. "Then what are we?"

I knew if I wanted to find you I had to escape. Then I would come back for the other boys. I figured out I could hide in one of the trucks that came and went through the day and see where it would take me. On the day I decided to do just that, Zaid called us all together. He said Nasir—the older Nasir, since there were several Nasirs—had run away by hiding in the back of a pickup truck.

"Where was he going in this desert?" Zaid said. "To visit the scorpions? To have dinner with the vultures? No, wait, he *was* the dinner for the vultures! My men found him still in the truck, dead, while the vultures ate out his eyeballs. This was all that was left of him!" He dropped a dirty white tunic on the sand. A black stain curved around one fold. "Any of you want to join him, go on! Your families do not want you. This land is not your land, so *they* do not want you—unless you care for their precious camels, their ships in the desert. You decide!"

He walked away. The boys circled the clothes. Youssef went closer and crouched down next to the tunic.

"Looks like blood," he said.

Slowly the boys walked away.

Youssef and I walked back to our shelter together.

"Do you think we will ever leave this place?" he asked.

"Yes, I am sure of it," I said.

"Alive?"

"Of course," I said, although I was not certain.

That night I realized the only way I could get to you was by being able to attend the races where all the other camel kids would be. I had to figure out a way to convince Zaid to let me become a jockey. Not that I wasn't terrified of that idea, Umar. Every day a child fell off and got hurt. Talat fell off a couple of times but was somehow unharmed. He curled into a ball before he hit the ground and he broke nothing. I don't know why. As the boys got more experience, they fell off less— until the trainer decided to speed the camels up; then the falls increased again.

A boy fell off not too long ago, and the camels trampled him. It was so horrible I can hardly bear to think of it. I did not see him fall, but I saw the men run to pick him up. He bounced around in their arms like a doll, his body limp and ragged. I don't know where they took him, but we all knew he was dead. That night after my story, each boy said his name out loud.

Then we were silent for a long while, sitting together, until one by one, the boys left the circle.

The best way for me to become a jockey was to figure out how I could get a camel to run faster when I was on it. As I said, the camels already liked me. I had learned right away that the camels were intelligent. They rewarded those who treated them well and punished those who did not. Several of the boys regularly scavenged from the men's area, so I asked them to bring back anything that boy or camel would eat. Each camel had its own likes and dislikes, and I encouraged the boys to try and find out what their camels most liked. It was obvious the trainers and owners—whoever they were—prized their camels and thought little of us, so if the camels were attached to us, perhaps we would have an easier time of it. At least this was what I believed.

In our barn, the queen of camels was Jaja. She had once been the hope of her owner, Zaid said. A few months ago, she hurt her leg. The leg got better, but she didn't want to race anymore. Lately she had started trying to bite her jockeys during the practice races. Zaid cursed her, hit her, threatened her. She tried to bite him; when that didn't work, she threw up on him.

When she was not racing, Jaja was gentle as a well-fed kitten. She followed me around and nibbled on my pockets looking for treats. Once I figured out that Jaja liked orange and lemon rinds, I whispered, "Rinds," every time I fed her. Soon I had only to say the word, and she would trot over to me from across the barn. Or I would stand next to her and whisper, "Rinds. Trough." And she would lope over to the trough. When I went to get her from the track, I practiced saying, "Rinds and trough," to see if that made her hurry back to the barn, and it did.

One day while I was brushing her, she turned her head as if to bite me, but I gave her a rind from my pocket and she turned back to the trough. I gently moved the hair away from the spot where I had just brushed, near her hump, and I found a bump with pus coming out of it. It was slightly calloused, so it must have been there for a while—and it was where the strap went around the hump.

I ran to Zaid to tell him. He hurried to the barn to

examine Jaja. The next day a man and a woman came to the barn to care for Jaja. The woman was white and wore the clothes of a Westerner.

She stood on a stool to look at the sore. "Keep her head still," the woman yelled in English.

As the woman poked and prodded her back, Jaja shook away the boys at her head. Finally I went over to Jaja and put several rinds and a date in my palm and held it out to her. She ate it all, looking at me while the woman leaned over her hump.

"Good girl," the woman said as she got down. For a moment of terror I thought she was speaking to me— had she discovered my secret? Then I realized she was talking to the camel.

"She'll be fine," the woman said. "Put this oint-ment on it three times a day. Why don't you let him, the boy with the scar—what's your name?" She was looking at me.

"Akbar," I said.

"Let Akbar do it," she said. "She seems to trust him. Don't put a saddle on her until it clears up."

She dropped a small jar into Zaid's hand, then left

with the other man. It was the first time I had seen a woman in weeks—months? I ran after her as she walked to her truck.

"Have you seen my brother Umar?" I asked her in English.

She stopped and looked at me.

"Your brother Umar? Where would I have seen him?"

"In one of the camel camps. He's about six years old."

She laughed. "Honey, I've seen dozens of boys who fit that description."

She opened the door to the pickup and got in. She waved at me, and they drove away.

Jaja's sore got better, but she still did not like being ridden.

"Let me try," I said to Zaid. "I bet I can get her to go farther than any of the other jockeys."

"Which would not be such a feat, since the stupid animal will only run a short distance!" he said.

Zaid finally agreed to let me ride Jaja. She seemed so tall, and I felt so tiny once I was on her hard and bony back. I was glad I had put on the sand pouch in anticipation of this moment. Jaja and I walked around for a while. She did not try to bite me. She started trotting. Ouch! That was not pleasant. I whispered, "Rind. Trough." She began running around the track. I held on very tightly! I thought for certain I would fall off. She passed by camel after camel while I rocked from side to side.

Soon we were back at the starting point. Jaja knelt down, and I slid off her back and quickly fed her an orange rind.

"You were only supposed to walk her!" Zaid said, slapping me across the back of my head.

"Ouch!" I said, rubbing my head. He did not hit me very hard, however, so I knew he was pleased.

After that, I rode Jaja nearly every day. Youssef was riding now, too. Trainers from other camps brought their camels and boys to our camp for practice races. I looked for you in the groups of new boys, but you were not there. I asked the boys if any of them knew a boy named Umar. No one did.

I rode Jaja during the practice races. We lined up at the starting line, someone shot off a gun, and we all

lurched forward. It seemed so crowded with all the
other camels and boys, and I was sure Jaja felt the same
way because she didn't even need to hear "rind." She
hurried to the head of pack and beyond. I felt as though
I were flying, Umar! I was terrified I would fall off, but
Jaja responded to my voice and the pressure from my
foot. I didn't need to use the whip—which meant I had
one more hand to use to cling to the strap. Trucks
drove around the outside of the track with men leaning
out of them, shouting at their jockeys and camels. Jaja
and I ignored it—ignored them all—and for a moment,
I imagined I was a Bedouin, traveling the deserts looking for adventures.

Soon it was time for the camel races outside the
city—wherever the city was. That was where I would
find you, Umar, I was certain. Not all of us could go.
Some of the boys had to stay behind with the camels in
training—including Shadow Boy. On the night before
we were to leave, the boys and I gathered together for
one last night of stories.

"Will you tell us what happened to Shahrazad?"
Shadow Boy asked.

"But you know what happened to her," I said. "All right. Let us talk of Shahrazad. Because his first wife had betrayed him, the King took a new wife for only a night, every night. At the end of the night, he would have someone kill the wife. Then he would pick another woman to be his bride. The entire kingdom lived in fear. Soon they would have no women left. Shahrazad stepped forward and asked her father to arrange for the King to make her his next bride. Her father begged her to reconsider, but she knew what she was doing. The King and Shahrazad got married and spent the night together. Afterward, she asked if she could tell a story to her sister before she met her fate. He agreed. She told the story and started another one. The King wanted to hear the end of the story, so he agreed to keep her another night as she told another story and another. Until one thousand and one nights had passed and she had told story after story and birthed three babies."

"Have you told one thousand and one stories?" one of the boys asked.

"No, nor have I birthed three babies."

The boys laughed.

"So what happened?"

"One night Shahrazad said, 'I have now told you tales for one thousand nights and one night. May I ask of you a favor?' The King said, 'Ask it.' 'Bring me my children,' she said. And her three boy children were brought to her. 'King, these are your children as they are mine. Will you spare my life so that they may not be motherless?' The King said, 'I pardoned you before these children were ever born because I knew you to be a good woman.' Soon the entire kingdom was celebrating the news. The King sent for his chroniclers, and they wrote down all the stories his wife had told and they named the compilation *The Stories of the Thousand Nights and A Night*. Praise be to Allah. And that is all."

The boys were silent. I wished then I could let them know that I was a woman. I wished I was dressed in something beautiful and colorful, that I could embrace each and every one of them and promise that their lives would be better. But I could not reveal myself or promise them.

"Remember," I said instead. "The nights are yours."

The boys walked up to me one at a time, put their

hands together at their hearts, and filed by. Shadow Boy was the last to leave. I stood and looked into his eyes. He was no longer Shadow Boy.

"Ibrahim," I said. "It is now up to you."

"You will be back," he said.

"That is not my wish," I said.

"Then it shall not be my wish," he said. "May Abu Hasan never come your way."

"Nor yours," I said. And we shook hands.

Then he walked away.

The morning was very difficult. Suleiman and Malik were staying behind too. Zaid had wanted Malik to go in Youssef's stead, but I begged him not to separate the brothers. I promised if Jaja did not win every race he entered us in Zaid could beat me senseless, but "please let Suleiman and Malik stay together." He grew weary of my entreaties and relented, but now we had to say good-bye to the brothers. I had no words. I hugged them tightly and gave them my needles and thread to hold on to. I hoped I would be back for the boys, but I could not promise.

The men loaded the camels onto trailers. The boys

and I, along with the men, got into the back of several pickups. If we had been alone, I would have told a story, but when the men were around, we pretended we were all stupid boys so that they would ignore us.

We reached our new home just before sunset. We had little time to get the camels unloaded and into the open barns before it was dark. We had to sleep out on the sand until dawn. As the sun came up, I saw the tents that would be home for a time. I was glad that our boys would all be together: We would not have to fight off other boys like we had had to at the beginning. I could see other camel camps and barns in the near distance; farther away was the racetrack.

It was several days before I had a chance to look for you, Umar. Youssef and I ran from camp to camp— which was no easy task given the distance and the chance we would get caught. We did not find you. We could not go to every camp, and I hoped I would see you at the races themselves.

We trained every morning from dawn to night, taking a break only when it was too hot. Two days before opening day, Zaid had us put something over each camel's mouth to prevent it from eating. I had to keep Jaja very still and calm.

On opening day, we went to the racetrack. So many people! Men with clipboards walked around talking to the trainers and owners. I looked for you every chance I got. Near to the tracks, a huge white tent stood over a bright green lawn with palm trees and shrubs growing around it. Colorfully clothed women stood together inside the tent on one side, men on the other. Behind the tent, I saw several shops, a mosque, maybe a police station.

Youssef ran over to me. "Have you seen Talat?" he asked.

"No," I said. "He went with his camel earlier. Why?"

"He seemed too scared," Youssef said. "This is his first real race."

"He did all right in the practice races," I said. I glanced at Youssef as he looked around at the camels, men, and boys. I wondered if he was frightened too.

"I thought my father might have come," Youssef said.

"Maybe he is here but hasn't found you yet," I said. "If he is, will you ask him to take you home?"

"Yes," he said. "I will have him take all three of us home."

When it was time, the boys and camels in my race lined up at the start. Trucks, cars, buses, and vans with television cameras idled on the other side of the fence, waiting for us to begin. Zaid had put something in my ear that allowed me to hear what the driver of the truck told me to do: Use the whip, use my heel, slow down, speed up. But Jaja and I had raced before, and I knew she would run faster than the rest just to get away from everything and everyone.

I heard the gun go off. Jaja jumped forward. We stayed with the other camels and riders as we raced past the tent and into the desert. The racetrack went for four kilometers and then curved back four more kilometers. Jaja eventually took the lead, and we were all alone for another kilometer. Suddenly the rocking motion became jerky. Jaja was limping! I pulled her to the side of the racetrack. She slowly sank to the sand, and I slipped off. Zaid got out of the truck, cursing as he hurried toward Jaja.

"She hurt her leg," I said.

He pushed me out of the way as the other camels ran by us. Two other men got out of the truck. They poked and prodded Jaja. She hollered for me, and I went to her head and fed her orange rinds. A camel van drove onto the track. Jaja stood and one of the men led her up the ramp and into the vehicle.

"You, go," Zaid said.

I jumped onto the truck with Jaja and held on to her rope as the truck slowly drove away.

Sometime later we stopped. The Western woman from the desert came to the van and told the men how to get Jaja into the building without hurting her. I stayed nearby and stroked her face as we went inside what looked like a brand-new hospital. Umar, you won't believe this: It was a hospital for camels! They took Jaja to a room that was nicer than anything I had ever seen. The Western woman did something to Jaja so that she fell asleep. I was allowed to leave then, while the woman, Zaid, and a man in white talked about Jaja.

I waited in a room nearby that had magazines, a television, and snacks. Since no one was around, I quickly ate some breads, a banana, and an orange. I stuffed a few pieces of the sweets and two fruits in my pocket for Talat and Youssef. I flipped through the magazines, but I could not read the script. Then I lay on the couch and fell asleep.

"Well, if it isn't scar-face," I heard someone say. I opened my eyes and quickly sat up. The Western woman stood next to a beautiful woman dressed in shimmering gold. I had to blink and wipe my eyes to see if I was dreaming.

"Scar-face," the Western woman said in English, "this is the Sheikha. Her husband owns all that you see, including you and the camels."

The Sheikha looked over at the woman, and the woman purposefully closed her mouth and circled her thumb and finger around her lips.

"How are you, young man?" the Sheikha said in English. "What is your name?"

"I am Ali Akbar," I said, standing. "I am honored to meet you."

"Your English is very good," the Sheikha said. "You are Jaja's jockey? You did very well. Someone else might have beaten her to keep her going until she crossed the finish line. As it is, she will be able to race again in two weeks' time."

"That is good to hear," I said.

"You will ride Jaja in the Sheikha's race then," the Sheikha said. "For the winning jockey, I grant any wish. Just like a jinni!" She laughed and her laugh sounded like water over stones. Soothing and joyful. I was tempted to get on my knees then and there and confess all to her and ask for her help in getting you back. But then I remembered her husband owned our camels— and the tiny camel kids.

"It would be good for someone like you to win," the Sheikha said. "It would put to rest all those rumors about us using underage children as jockeys. I look forward to seeing you in two weeks if you are the winner. Last year the young boy asked for ice cream. I hope you will ask for something more interesting."

"If I am the winner," I said, "I promise to ask for something interesting."

The Sheikha and the Western woman left. Zaid stepped out of the shadows and slapped me on the back of the head.

"So the Sheikha has a favorite, does she?" Zaid said. "You best not disappoint her."

I returned to camp by nightfall. Talat and Youssef were asleep in our tent but awakened when I came inside. I gave them the treats I had saved.

"I am so sore," Youssef said.

"Me too," Talat said. "Some of the other kids whipped me."

"No! When? Why?" I asked.

"When we were racing," Talat said. "They wanted me to fall off the camel."

Youssef nodded. "You're lucky you were on a winner."

"Not quite," I said. "They weren't our boys whipping you, were they?"

"No, from the other camps," Youssef said.

"I found out that in two weeks there's the Sheikha's Race. The winning jockey can ask for anything he wants! If I win, I will ask the Sheikha to find my brother."

"If I win, I will ask the Sheikha to find your brother," Talat said.

"If I win, I will ask the Sheikha to find your brother."

"Oh!" I said. "You are so kind. You are my brothers,

153

too. I would never leave this place without you."

We were silent in the darkness.

Then Youssef cleared his throat.

"Ali Akbar," he said, "Talat, Suleiman, and Malik asked me to speak with you about this before we left, but it is only now that I am able to do it."

"What is it?" I asked.

Youssef cleared his throat again.

Talat leaned closer to me and whispered, "We know you're a girl."

I was stunned, Umar. I did not know what to say.

"How?" I asked.

"Well, your chest when you race . . ."

"Oh no," I said. "What if someone else has seen?"

"If someone else had seen you would probably not be here," Youssef said. "We already suspected since . . . since you bleed like my sister bleeds."

"I told you it was from riding the camels," I said.

"But it happened before you rode the camels," Youssef said. "You have to find a way to leave here before they catch you. We would not be able to protect you."

"I know," I said. "But I have to find my brother."

"You will do your brother no good if you are dead," Youssef said.

"All right," I said. "I will stay until the Sheikha's Race. If I don't find my brother by then, I will figure out a way to leave."

"I knew you were a girl because you hugged me like my mother used to," Talat whispered.

"The way she will again," I said.

At the Races

DURING THE NEXT TWO DAYS of racing, Zaid allowed me to do what I pleased. I don't know why. Every once in a while he shouted at me to get to work, but I would run away and look through the crowds for you, Umar. Face after face. Little boy after little boy.

I was fairly certain I could find a way to get to the tent and steal clothes from some woman's bags in case I had to escape. No one pays much attention to little dark boys here. They are like grains of sand.

During the two days of races, too many boys fell off the camels and got hurt. A doctor of sorts gave the boys pills when they cried out and set broken arms and legs. I carried water to the boys during the day and tried to make certain they were drinking enough.

"You will make them fat!" Zaid said.

"Would you rather have them dead?" I said. "Water will keep them more alert and they will sweat it off or pee it out."

After one of his races, Youssef told me, "You must not make Zaid angry or he might start to question you— or make you take off your shirt so he can beat you."

He was right, so I made myself less conspicuous. When the races were over for the weekend, we returned to our nearby camp. Jaja soon came back from the camel hospital. I walked, groomed, massaged, and fed her. After several days, Zaid declared she was fit to race.

The two weeks went by quickly, and we returned to the track for the first day of races. The Sheikha's Race was not until the next day, so I was free to help Youssef and Talat, who were both racing today: Talat first, then Youssef.

"Did you ever tell Zaid about the other boys whipping you?" I asked them.

Youssef said, "Yes, and he told me that would teach me to be a loser."

When it was time, Youssef and I watched Talat on his camel, waiting at the starting line. He glanced back at us. I smiled.

Then the gun went off, and the camels and trucks lurched forward. We watched until we could not see and then until the dust cleared and we were certain we could not see. We ran to one of the TV monitors to watch. Poor Talat's camel was stuck in the middle of the pack. I couldn't see Talat for a minute. The camels began to move away from one another. But Talat wasn't there. His camel was riderless.

I gasped. Youssef ran to one of the trucks and shouted something to the driver. He hopped in the back, and they drove away. I found the doctor—or whatever he was—and we waited for the truck to return. Within minutes it came racing up to us in a cloud of dust. I heard Talat screaming before I saw him.

"Talat!" I yelled, running to the back of the truck. "Fix him! Fix him!"

Tears streamed down his cheeks, but Talat was

alive. He was moving and crying. The doctor pulled on his arm as he held on to his shoulders. Talat screamed.

"His shoulder was dislocated," the doctor said. "He will be fine now."

He left, and I picked up Talat and carried him away to a quiet patch of desert.

"You're safe," I said. Youssef patted the back of his head. "You are safe."

Thirty minutes later, Talat seemed to have forgotten his injury. I found him something cold to drink, and we sat on the sand waiting for Youssef's race.

"Cheer for me," Youssef said as he left us to go saddle up. "It will be like family is here!"

"Your family is here," I said. "We are your family, brother. Go claim your victory."

He hurried away.

"Do you want to get closer so we can see better?" I asked Talat.

He nodded. I took Talat's hand, and we walked through the crowds to get closer to the race. I heard the gun go off. The camels surged forward, slowly at first. They soon bunched together.

"I don't like when they do that," Talat said. "They get too close."

"I know," I said.

Suddenly, one of the camels broke free from the pack—only she was coming our way, the wrong way, and she was riderless.

"Youssef," I whispered.

I let go of Talat's hand and raced onto the track. Several men tried to grab the rope of the camel. I ran past them, toward a spot of color in the sand—a spot the camels kept running over. A spot the camels kept trampling over. Forever, it seemed. Over and over. The spot of color bouncing as the hooves pummeled it. Or maybe it was a delusion. Or a hallucination. I felt like I was in a dream and I could not run fast enough and I could not scream loud enough and I kept calling Youssef's name over and over . . .

. . . and when I reached Youssef's side, when I reached his side, when I sank into the sand next to him, it was as though he were asleep—like all those other times I had seen him sleeping, only this time a drop of blood sealed his lips, like wax on an ancient letter. Just one drop. And I knew Youssef was not asleep. He was not injured. He was dead. I screamed. And wept. Then I leaned over and kissed his lips and sent him on his way.

After the Races

I DON'T REMEMBER MUCH about the rest of the day. That night Talat and I lay together in our tent. His arm hurt, but he did not cry. He wiped my tears. Every time I closed my eyes, I saw Youssef in the sand. It was my fault he was here. Zaid had wanted to leave him behind. Take Malik. But I had argued with him. Me. It was not my place to argue. It was not my place to be here.

I had one more chance to make it right. Just one.

In the morning, Zaid said Talat would have to ride again since they were short two jockeys.

"He hurt his arm," I said.

"He is fine," Zaid said.

"No, he is not," I said. "Touch his arm and he will scream."

"That is because you baby him! It is his job to ride, and he will ride."

I looked from Zaid to Talat and back again.

"Then I will not ride Jaja," I said.

"Then I will beat you," he said.

"I still won't ride," I said, "and the Sheikha will wonder where I am. She might even send for me and I would have to tell her how you treat your jockeys."

Zaid put his face close to mine. "You think they don't know what goes on here? You are stupid, then!"

"If Talat does not ride, I will ride," I said. "If he rides, I won't. Even if you tie me to the camel. I'll fall off—right as we're going past the Sheikha."

Zaid growled. Then he said, "If you do not win, I will beat you both until you beg to die."

It was strange to be at the racetrack without Youssef. The other boys missed him, too. I tried to talk with each of them and encourage them to stay alert—and alive. I looked at the face of every new boy I saw, but you were not there, Umar! It was finally time for my race. Jaja seemed anxious to go. Before I got on her, I let her smell my pocket so she knew I had treats waiting for her.

We got in line. The gun went off. The camels surged forward. These were the fastest camels from all over. Everyone wanted to win the Sheikha's prize. The winning trainer and jockey (and owner if the winning camel did not belong to the Sheikh) got all kinds of prizes. I only wanted my wish granted.

First we had to win. The camels moved as a group. Zaid screamed in my ear. "Get out of there! Get out!" I pulled the ear piece off. Several camels—including Jaja—moved ahead of the pack. I felt something slice into my back. I glanced behind me to the left. A boy held up a whip. I reached for it as it came down on my back again. That's when I saw the other jockeys behind me. That was when I recognized one of the faces: tired, dirty, and intent. The face of my beloved brother. You, Umar. I had finally found you.

I wanted to scream with joy, but the boy started whipping me again. Jaja surged forward then. I let her go ahead. I kept glancing back to see if you were safe—although you had not seen me yet. The camels made the turn and the whipping boy was there again. Jaja seemed content to be away from the crowd but next to the whipping boy. I glanced back once more at you, Umar, but I knew I still had to win because now my wish would be for the Sheikha to send my brother Umar and me home.

I whispered, "Rind. Trough." Jaja jumped forward and left the whipping boy behind as we raced toward the finish line a kilometer or so ahead. The whipping boy caught up with us once again, and I murmured, "Rind! Rind!"

Jaja and I crossed the finish line first. I could hear the cheers and see the boys jumping up and down. Someone grabbed a hold of Jaja. I quickly slipped down and watched for the other camels. One by one they hurried over the finish line. I watched for you, Umar. And watched.

Then a riderless camel trotted over the finish line. And you were nowhere. I started running down the track. No, no, no! This couldn't happen. Not now. Not now. After all we had been through. After all I had seen, I had to save my little brother.

I ran down the track and into the dust.

"Umar!" I shouted.

I wished for a jinni to blow away the dust so that I might find you safe.

And then a boy walked through the sand, helmet in hand.

"Umar!" I screamed.

You looked up and saw me then and started running toward me. You were safe! You were not injured! I ran to you and scooped you up into my arms and held you next to me, held you so tight I could feel your heart beating next to mine, and you whispered, "I knew you would come, sister. I knew it."

(This part you know, Umar.
So I will write it to Ami.)

ZAID RAN OVER TO ME, CURSING
and swearing. He told me to hurry over to the Sheikha,
who was awaiting me. I kept Umar's hand tightly in
mine as we walked. A man approached us, and Umar
hid behind me.

"Give me that child!" the man said.

"You will not have him," I said.

The man reached for Umar. Suddenly he was surrounded by dozens of boys.

I repeated, "You will not have him."

The man moved away.

We walked to where the Sheikha and Sheikh stood
near a microphone and television cameras. I felt like I

was in a dream again. I had difficulty focusing on anything except Umar's hand in mine. The Sheikh pre-
sented the man in white with a check and keys to a
car. He gave cash to Zaid. Then the Sheikha turned to
me and said, "Ahhh, Ali Akbar, I see you have won the
race! Now what interesting wish would you like me to
grant you?"

I looked down at Umar. He smiled.

"This is my brother Umar," I said. "And we would
like to go home now."

The Sheikh laughed and started talking to someone
next to him. The cameras moved away. A moment later,
the Sheikh strode over to Umar and me and said, "You
are now my best jockey. I cannot let you go! I will send
your brother home, but no, you must stay here. We will
make certain your family is well provided for. Jaja is my
favorite camel, and you are her favorite jockey."

The Sheikh turned and moved away with the
crowd. The Sheikha started to go with her husband
when I said, "Sheikha, I beg you. I must speak with
you alone."

"Don't bother the Sheikha," Zaid said. "Come with me."

"No, please," I said.

"Leave him be," the Sheikha said. "Take the little boy and I will speak with Ali Akbar."

"No, my brother must come too," I said.

"Very well," she answered.

Umar and I followed the Sheikha as she walked to a long black car. Someone opened the door for her, and she got in.

"Come, come," she said to us.

Umar and I climbed in after her.

"I apologize for our untidiness," I said.

She laughed. The car went forward for a few minutes and then stopped. We got out and stepped up into a big bus. Inside was a beautiful apartment. It was like dropping into Aladdin's lamp. It was so plush and colorful—with mirrors, cushions, and cords of gold. Several women stood as the Sheikha walked into the apartment.

"May I speak with you alone?" I asked.

"No!" one of the women said.

"What an impish child!" another said.

"Leave us," the Sheikha said. "Take the little boy

into the next room and feed him something."

I let Umar's hand go. "No," he said.

"They're just going into that room," the Sheikha pointed. "See that window? You can look through it the entire time you're eating."

"It's all right," I said. "No one will separate us now."

The women led Umar away. I watched him from my seat next to the Sheikha.

"I must plead with you to ask the Sheikh to let me go," I said. "I don't want to embarrass you or the Sheikh, but it will eventually come to light, and I'm afraid it could cause me to lose my life and your husband to lose respect."

"What is it?" the Sheikha asked.

I leaned over and picked up a red scarf from the back of a chair. I wrapped it around my head and let it fall over my shoulders.

"My name is Nadira," I said. "My brother was kidnapped and brought here to work as a camel jockey. No one was doing anything to get him back, so I disguised myself as a boy and came to rescue him. Today, I found him. I also found many other boys who have been horribly mistreated. They've been starved, beaten, and sexually assaulted. Many of them fall from the camels and are injured or killed."

The Sheikha watched me silently. After a moment, she said, "I must have proof that you are who you claim to be."

I pulled my tunic in the back so that it was tight in the front. She glanced at my breasts.

Then she got on the phone.

"Ask the Sheikh to come here immediately," she said.

We sat in silence, waiting. Soon the door opened, and the Sheikh stepped into the apartment on wheels. He looked at his wife, then whispered to the men with him and they left. I could still see Umar. He waved and I waved back.

The Sheikh sat next to his wife.

"Tell him," she said.

"Do you know the story of Shahrazad?" I asked.

"Certainly," he said, frowning.

"I would ask a favor of you," I said. "If you find my story interesting and compelling, will you send my brother and me home?"

The Sheikh leaned back and put his arms up across the back of the couch.

"I will strike that bargain," he said. "Proceed."

"In June of this year, my brother Umar was kidnapped from the streets outside the hovel my mother has been living in since before she became a widow," I said. "I was working for Begum Naseem as a maid and a cook."

The Sheikha sat forward.

"My name is Nadira," I said, "and this is what has happened since then."

I told him the entire story. He did not say a word. The Sheikha gasped several times, and once she dabbed away tears. When I finished speaking, the Sheikh was quiet for a moment. He held my fate in his hands. I thought of Youssef and Talat, Shadow Boy and the others. He held all of our fates in his hands.

Finally he said, "This is an interesting tale. And I find it honorable and true. I will send you and your brother home, if you will help me first."

"Anything," I said.

"We will call this Mr. Bashir," he said, "and we will

find the camp you came from and rescue the boys."

"There are many boys right here," I said. "We could send them to the rehabilitation center tonight."

The Sheikh nodded. Then he stood and said loudly, "Now get out of those clothes! You look like a boy!"

Soon After

THE WOMEN BATHED UMAR AND me—separately, of course. They put oil on me, as though I were a bride. Then they brought me lovely blue pants and an orange tunic. The scarf they wrapped around my head was the most beautiful thing I had ever seen—aside from Umar's dirty tear-streaked face. The scarf was the color of moonlight.

Afterward, I returned to the racetrack with the Sheikh and Sheikha. Talat ran up and embraced me. I introduced him to Umar. Soon he and Umar were inseparable. All the boys got on a bus—including me. They took us to Bashir's rehabilitation center. I wished

so much that Youssef had been with us. What a difference twenty-four hours could make!

A few days later, we searched the desert for the
camp. After several false tries, we found the boys. They
ran up to the car, cheering. None of them seemed the
least bit surprised that I was a woman. We took them
all back to Bashir's.

On the night before Umar and I were to leave for
home, I asked Ibrahim to help me make masala chai, and
so we did. Then I sat in the chair the boys had placed at
the head of the room, and they sat around me. Ibrahim
brought me a cup of masala chai. I took it from his
hands and smiled; all signs of Shadow Boy were entirely
gone. I looked around the room as Ibrahim and Bashir
served the boys. Umar and Talat sat closest to me.

"This masala chai recipe is my mother's, Bibi
Mariam," I said. "Masala chai is an ancient drink from
thousands of years ago. The King thought so highly of
his recipe that he kept it hidden. Many believed true
masala chai was healing and helped promote immortality.
Bandits broke into the King's treasury and stole the

recipe. But when they made the masala chai, they did not feel any healthier or live any longer. This was because the King had changed the recipe just slightly to fool the bandits. Ever since then, people have been altering the recipe, trying to find the original. Let's hope this is it."

We sipped our masala chai.

"A story," Malik said. The other boys clapped. I nodded.

"There was once a group of boys who were stolen from all over the country," I began. "They suffered many hardships. They encountered many monsters—worse than any Sindbad had seen! Some of them did not survive. Some of them fell into the charnel cave as Sindbad did and forgot their way for a time. But in the end, they came together and protected one another until it was time to go home and be with their families again."

"I don't know where home is," one of the boys said.

"I know," I said. "We will do everything we can to help you."

"I have another story," Ibrahim said, looking at the boys. "It is about Shahrazad. You have heard she had a sister. But let me tell you, she had a brother, too. When he was taken by bandits, she cut her locks and put away her beautiful clothes and followed the bandits. They were no match for her. Her cheek had been kissed by the moon because the moon knew she was more clever and beautiful than anyone alive! She rescued her brother along with all the other boys who had been kidnapped. She will forever be their sister!"

The boys cheered and clapped.

"And you," I said, "you will all be my brothers. Forever."

UMAR AND I HAD A WARM AND wonderful reunion with our Ami. She was so happy. She wanted us next to her all the time. Umar had many bad nights when we got home. He told me some of what happened to him but not all. Bashir and his wife are setting up a rehabilitation center here, too. He has asked me to help, and I have agreed.

A few weeks after we got home, Begum Naseem and her husband made a great feast for us. Noor and her new husband came. We invited the man at the flower shop who had been kind enough to track down my mother and give her the green book. Some of the boys who had been with me or Umar at our respective camel training camps had already been repatriated, and they attended our party with their parents.

When Talat arrived, he stood at the entrance to the room for a moment looking shyly around. Then he saw me and ran straight into my arms. I held him so tightly neither of us could breathe! Then he and Umar went off to play with Duri on his computer. The house was full of people and music and food. It was even better than a wedding feast. My mother and Saliq's father seemed to have gotten closer while I was gone. I wondered if they would marry soon.

During the party, my mother took me aside and handed me a package wrapped in bright yellow paper. I carefully took the paper off a dark green box. I lifted the cover off the box. Inside lay a copy of *A Thousand Nights and One Night.*

"Oh, Ami!" I said. I lifted the book up and opened it.

"'To my beloved son. Remember Shahrazad, and always learn wisely,'" I read. "Ami! It's Baba's copy. How did you get it?"

"Your father sold it to Rubel. Not that Rubel ever read it. I said he had to give me back everything your father had sold him or I was turning him over to the police for selling Umar. I found this book amongst the returns."

I hugged my mother. "Thank you, Ami."

"Now, I must get back to our guests," she said. "You, too."

Later in the evening, Saliq and I stepped outside together. We stood under the same moon we had stood under so many months earlier, when I cried by the pond. Everything else was different now.

"When I first came home and you saw me," I said, "your eyes filled with tears."

"I was so happy to know you were safe and well," he said. "We had all been so worried about you. Especially your mother. And me."

We stood by the pond for a moment in silence.

"I think the flower vendor has an eye on my mother," I said. "You better tell your father to watch out."

Saliq laughed, then cleared his throat. He sounded like Youssef.

"What is it?" Saliq asked. "You look like you're going to cry."

"I was thinking of Youssef," I said. "The young man who died."

"I'm so sorry," he said.

"I think he would have grown into a good man," I said. "He was a good boy."

I reached into my pockets and pulled out the green and red books I had written in. "Remember Shahrazad" and "Learn Wisely." I handed them to Saliq.

"I want you to read these," I said. "Then return them to me."

"I am honored," he said.

"You should be."

He laughed. "You're different than before."

Now I laughed.

"That didn't make much sense, did it?" he said. "I'm nervous. I want to ask you to be my wife, but I don't know how. I mean, should I get a marriage broker? Should I talk to your mother?"

"You are an odd person," I said.

He nodded sadly.

"I like that about you," I said. "But you don't have to ask anyone about marrying me because I don't want to get married."

"You don't?"

"No. I don't want a man telling me what to do," I said.

"What if I promise I won't ever tell you what to do?" he asked.

"I don't want someone fussing about me working with Bashir or anyone else," I said. "I want to help those children."

"Maybe I want to help with you," he said.

"The Sheikh has offered to pay for an operation to remove the scar on my face," I said. "I haven't decided what I'll do yet. It feels different now, like it's not a scar. It's a mark that has nothing to do with those men in the village. We'll see."

"How about this," Saliq said. "If I tell you an interesting story and in the end you agree it is interesting, will you then marry me?"

"Hmmm," I said. "We'll see."

"Nadira!" Umar ran out of the house toward me. "Nadira, come. The boys want to hear a story, and they're calling for you."

Umar grabbed my hand. I knelt down so our faces were opposite each other.

"Umar, you never told me what the kidnappers said to get you to go with them," I said.

"They said my sister was in trouble and needed my help."

"Oh, Umar," I said, embracing him.

After a moment he pulled away and said, "Before we go inside, I want to see the moon."

I pointed to the one overhead. "There it is," I said.

"No, not that one."

I moved my scarf away from my cheek so he could see it. Umar leaned over and kissed the scar.

"Does it hurt anymore?" he asked.

"Not a bit," I said.

I stood and took his hand. Umar grabbed Saliq's hand and the three of us went back into the house, where my mother was passing out masala chai.

"I changed the recipe a bit," she said as she handed me a cup. "This just might be the original recipe. You never know."